Doctor Fix-It

A Doctors of Eastport General Hospital Novel

Mel Walker

To everyone who are doing their best to navigate the rules while building the plane as you fly.

Contents

Chapter One

D *addy would not approve.*

The silly line causes me to giggle into my vodka tonic, the same mix I've just sent to a stranger sitting alone on the other side of the hotel bar. I raise a questioning brow at Eddie, the bartender, who knows my routine. Once a month, I drop all my inhibitions and let off a bit of steam at the one bar in Eastport, Rhode Island, I know I won't run into any of my hospital colleagues.

Eddie saunters over, his sleeves rolled up to his elbow, showcasing his dangerous tattoos. The ones that are a conversation starter for the shy female business travelers that frequent this hotel bar. Since I'm not a traveler, I'm immune to his spell.

Eddie leans over the counter, his green eyes sparkling in my direction, and I tip forward. "Sorry for the slim pickings tonight, Angie," he states with a devilish smile. He winks at the attractive blonde sitting two stools over from me. A shared smile, letting her know he's all hers in a minute. "There's a kiddie doll conference this week, hence the lack of testosterone tonight."

He may be apologizing to me, but his smirk tells me he's loving the switch-up. Eddie has made more cosmos, margaritas, and mojitos tonight than I've seen in the two-plus years I've been coming here. The bar is normally filled with traveling businessmen. Not tonight. The ratio is reversed, eighty percent women.

I run a finger across the rim of my drink. I don't care about the odds. I lift my glass and tip it toward the tall, dark stranger, who holds up my gift to him. A single brow raises as he takes a tentative sip. His gaze locks with mine, and I match his movement. The warmth of the alcohol spreads in my chest. I lower my drink, lips parting as a soft sigh escapes my lips. The stranger mirrors my movement, and the corners of his eyes crinkle in delight.

Let the games begin.

"All it takes is one. We good?" I whisper to Eddie while my gaze remains on the amused stranger.

A soft chuckle escapes Eddie's lips before he whips the bar rag off his shoulder and wipes in front of me, pulling my attention to him. "Yeah. He opened a tab. He's staying in the hotel. Don't know his story, but I got his info. You're good."

"Wish me luck," I joke and quirk my neck for the stranger to join me.

"Luck has nothing to do with what you are about to do," Eddie teases and strides toward the blonde.

I twist on the stool and uncross and cross my legs, my short black dress riding up my thigh. The movement serves its purpose, causing the approaching stranger to slow his steps and give me an opportunity to appreciate the view.

The man is tall, at least six feet, African American like me, his skin two shades darker than my sandy brown. Short Afro, thin mustache, strong jaw, and magnetic dark eyes unapologetically locked onto my legs. It's a look that only comes with experience, which lowers any anxiety I may feel. I made the mistake of picking up a twenty-something kid once. He never got the memo of how these things are supposed to work. It took nearly two months to pry his clingy hands away. Now I only target men closer to my age, mid-thirties, old enough to know better but smart enough not to care.

They, like me, understand the rules. Lonely doesn't always mean alone.

"You must be one of the models for the dolls at the conference. Tell me the name and I'll order a case right now." The timbre of his voice is intense, the deep melody causing vibrations in my chest I hadn't expected.

"If you tell me you play with dolls for a living, I'm turning and walking away," I tease, not really.

He steps into my personal space with confidence I find attractive. "Only living, breathing dolls such as yourself. I'm

Brayton—thank you for the drink. I can't recall the last time a woman sent one my way." His hand envelops mine, nearly swallowing it. Strong eye contact, a slightly sexy smirk on his lips. This close, I take in his stormy dark eyes, the ones assessing my every move. This is not his first rodeo. Good. I won't have to explain the rules to him.

I glance over his shoulder as he slips onto the barstool next to mine. "Figured I'd make the move before someone else beat me to it. I'm sure you've noticed..." I sweep a hand across the bar. "The odds certainly aren't in my favor tonight," I tease.

His gaze doesn't deviate from me for one second. It's a piercing, comforting gaze, a look of contentment on his handsome face. I feel the drumbeat in my chest. This man could prove dangerous to me and my rule. He takes his time, lets the sexual tension between us percolate before delivering his line with a certainty most men lack. "There is no competition for someone like you..."

"Angie." My real name slips out without a thought. This man is already chipping away at my rules. Never give them your real name. And thanks to mister twenty-something, never give them your phone number. "If you're not here for the doll conference, what brings you to our beautiful little town?"

A spark of joy flashed across his face, and I wonder what I said to elicit such a response. "Our?" He lets the word hang in the air, his lips ticking up into a dangerous smile. "So, I take it you live here?"

Shit.

I turn to hide in my drink. He's gotten more information out of me in a few heartbeats than I usually give after a few hours with a stranger. *What kind of spell are you weaving, Brayton?*

"Something like that." I take a long sip and ignore the movement next to me until I hear the familiar voice.

"How's everyone doing here?" Eddie directs the question at Brayton, but his gaze locks on me.

I give him a soft smile and nod. "As good as possible, thanks," I whisper, pleased in the whirlwind of Brayton, I am able to recite the code phrase Eddie devised for me.

The plastic in his smile melts to reveal a genuine Eddie grin. "I'll be around if you need anything," he says and works his way down the bar.

"You and the bartender?"

I turn to face Brayton with a furrowed brow. Curiosity and not attitude accompanies his question. I add perceptive to the list of traits he possesses, the list growing by the minute.

"Just a friend. We look out for each other." Another truth slips out, and I decide to stop fighting whatever it is that has my heart beating like a schoolgirl's.

"And what exactly is it that you are looking for?" He knows damn well what he is saying. He knows damn well what he is doing. His voice drops an octave, the deep vibration enough to pop open a younger woman's bra strap. His finger lands on the pulse point of my wrist. A slow sensuous stroke follows.

I won't back down. I'm not that woman. "I think we both know, and something tells me you are looking for the same thing." I capture his gaze and hold it tight like a pair of lucky dice at the casino. I skip over the list of questions in my playbook, skipping ahead to the one deal breaker, the one rule I've never broken and never will. "Are you married or in a serious relationship?" I hold his gaze and pray I'm as perceptive as him. I search for the hesitation, I search for the deceit, and all I find is a pair of dark eyes that carry with them a warmth that matches what I feel in my chest.

"Someone did that to me once." He reveals his truth, starting mid-story. I nod with familiarity. We are two broken souls seeking reassurance. "I like games, but I would never play that one." He then says the two words that close the deal. "No strings."

His last two words ring in my ears, my overstimulated mind interpreting them on more levels than I'm sure he even meant. Past, present, future.

I lean into Brayton, my lips an inch from his ear. My tongue flicks across his earlobe, and I whisper, "Close out your tab. I'll meet you by the elevator."

I don't wait for a response, merely stepping away. I slow my stride, secure in the knowledge his gaze is locked on me. Those stubborn five extra pounds that refuse to go away with age no longer bother me. I've discovered the secret after so many pitfalls—men are visual creatures, and I do all right in that department—but what they find irresistible is confidence. And I'm no longer the confused, heartbroken twenty-something-year-old studying sixteen hours a day through med school. I'm a grown woman who no longer waits around, hoping a man stumbles across her. I go out and get what I want.

And tonight, I want Brayton, and I don't care Daddy wouldn't approve.

Chapter Two

"**I** It's going to be that type of day," I mutter as I turn the corner and immediately spot the pharmaceutical sales rep from Droga Pharmaceuticals. Brittany, Barbara, or some close facsimile is her name, the reps all interchangeable blonde twenty-somethings with designer suits, artificial smiles, and clouds of perfume.

The joy of spending adult time with Brayton seems like a distant memory. I walked out of his hotel suite at four in the morning filled with more joy than I normally associate with a one-night stand. He backed up every bit of the confidence he possessed with skills I hadn't experienced in some time. But it wasn't just the sex that had me beaming. He did something few men do. He focused on me. A dozen tiny gestures told me he is a natural empath, concerned with the comfort and joy of others. Even when the night was coming to an end, he didn't force me out of my comfort zone.

"Brayton Patterson is my full name. I'm on Facebook and IG if you ever decide to break the rules." His statement was delivered with a sexy smile and no pressure, a combination that had my legs turning to rubber and my rule in danger of being destroyed. I made no promise, yet here I am, twelve hours later, and all I can think about is him.

"Dr. Carmichael, do you have a minute for me today? I have something for you." I step around the pharmaceutical rep, but not before I'm assaulted with the latest puff of fragrance from her. It's everything she wishes to be, sweet and strong.

She sticks a large blue-and-white gift certificate on top of the medical chart I'm carrying. The reps are relentless. They will try just about anything to entice a doctor to stop and spend more than thirty seconds with them so they can deliver their latest spiel on how their product is the next best thing in the world of medicine and I should immediately prescribe it to every one of my patients.

I make the mistake of pausing for a heartbeat to read the certificate. The blue-and-white gold-embossed heavy stock card advertises the Serenity Spa, the high-end spa that opened last year on Highland Boulevard less than a quarter of a mile from Eastport General Hospital.

"The certificate includes the sauna, massage, manicure, and pedicure. I can upgrade it for any other treatments you may wish." Barbie steps to me, her sky-blue eyes roaming across my face to my *didn't have much time to fix* hair. "I've heard wonderful things about their salon."

Ouch, do I look that bad? "Thanks, but no thanks..." I don't dare speak her name, which I know will be wrong. The reps change so often it's pointless to memorize their name. "Hospital policy and all. There is a whole reporting process..."

A lean hand sweeps across my clipboard and snatches the certificate. "I'm overdue for a manicure." I don't need to turn, the arrogance in the voice putting me on my heels.

"Dr. Morgan, to what do we owe the pleasure of you gracing the hallways of the Ortho Unit?"

"Now, Angie, I've told you a hundred times, you can call me Reggie," he starts, stepping between me and the sales rep.

"Well, I was taught to always refer to a fellow doctor by their proper name. Doctor Know-It-All I believe is yours."

Reggie steps close to me, close enough I smell the peppermint he's always popping. He's Caucasian, medium height, and wears a crisp white collared shirt with a sharp designer black tie underneath his lab jacket. Reggie is the chief physician in the emergency room and rarely ventures up to the sixth floor and the Ortho Unit.

"Ah, if we are going by pet names, I'll use yours, Doctor Stickler." He waves the certificate in front of my face like a red flag in front of a bull. "We all know how you are about sticking to the rules." He delivers the line with a smile, but it does little to lessen the sting. Reggie is one of the most talented doctors at Eastport General Hospital but loves to live on the edge. Me, I'm only thirty-three years old and don't have his track record, so I stick to every rule. Reggie knows my history and why I am the way I am, yet he slips in digs at every opportunity.

I tip to my side and peek at the sales rep, who continues to wait with a smile on her face as if she thinks she may have an opportunity to snag two doctors. "Apologies. I have a patient to see. Please be sure to register that certificate with the administration."

I turn but not before overhearing Dr. Morgan say, "Brooke, don't worry about the registration. I'll take care of it."

I shake my head and cut through the cluster of desks at the nurses' station, hoping to separate myself from both of them.

"Hold up, Angie. I came up to talk to you." I increase my pace, my patient's door ahead. "Doctor to doctor," he adds.

My feet halt, and I turn to face him. He waves the certificate in my direction. "You sure you don't want to join me? We could get a couple's massage." His blue-gray eyes twinkle in the fluorescent light. Reggie is nearly forty and should have outgrown these childish games, but he looks and acts ten years younger.

I can't deny the fact that he's a handsome man. The problem is he's well aware of this fact. I've seen ER residents and other doctors feeding his enormous ego. Even with all that attention, for some reason, he hits on me every opportunity he gets.

"I thought you said you were up here as a professional, not looking for your next Tinder hookup." I doubt he's on Tinder. A man like that gets swiped right just walking the halls of the hospital.

"If you're on there, I guess I should create a profile." I roll my eyes and turn. "Sorry, but you left that door open. You know you'd be disappointed if I didn't say something."

I place my palm on my patient's door. "Five seconds, Dr. Morgan. Some of us have patients to see."

The smile on his face fades. "So do I—that's why I'm here. I have someone in the ER with a sport-related injury. Baseball player, a kid, felt a pop and feared a break. His dad brought him in."

I step away from the doorway, intrigued. "Sounds simple enough. Why the rush up to Ortho?" I'm a specialist in orthopedics, but Dr. Morgan's knowledge in the area has impressed me on more than one occasion. He wouldn't have made the trek up this way if the case was simple.

He crosses his arms against his chest, and his lips go flat. "I have to show you the X-ray and a few other things. I ran a BMD, and it showed something odd. I need a formal consult."

I nod as my pulse begins to race. A BMD is a bone mineral density test. It measures the amount of calcium and bone minerals in the bone. It's not a test normally run for a break, let alone one run on a kid.

Intrigue races through my blood. I got into medicine because my father is a doctor. He was my hero growing up, saving lives, making a difference. I wanted to follow in his footsteps, only to discover medicine is not the black-and-white profession I had envisioned. Even after hundreds of years of recorded history, there remains so much unknown. Some days, I feel like a detective attempting to follow the clues and figure out a mystery. The relentless pursuit, the roller coaster of emotions of the near misses, the euphoria of solving the riddle. Defeating the illness and giving your patients their lives back intact is one of the greatest feelings in the world.

"Give me five minutes. I just have to discharge my patient. Meet you in the ER?" I begin to push the door and notice Dr. Morgan following me.

"It's been too long since I've seen you in action," he whispers and steps into the small hospital room.

I feel a pull on my elbow by Dr. Morgan stopping my progress as a skateboard races across the floor in front of me. One more step and I would have tripped over it. Reggie pulls me, my back landing against his hard chest just as a little boy of about eight years old races after the skateboard.

"Carter! I told you to sit." The frustrated voice of Marian Anderson, my patient, rolls off the boy's shoulder. She pushes herself up on the hospital bed with her one good arm, failing to use the bed harness that hangs overhead. Her eyes are rimmed in red, and her hair is pulled back in a messy bun.

Her son scoops up the board and giggles, as if skating indoors at a hospital is normal behavior. I turn and spot Marian's clueless husband, Darin. He's sitting on the lounge chair staring at his phone, their two-year-old daughter on his lap drooling apple juice down her chest onto her father's lap. I hear the loud empty slurps from across the room. She is sucking on air, and he fails to notice it. Not the only thing in the room he neglects.

"Maybe I will wait down in the ER with the gunshot victims. I think I'll be safer down there," Reggie jokes, attempting to distract me from the scene in front of me.

"Darin!" Marian screams at her husband. "Please, control the kids for two seconds. The doctor is here."

"It's fine. I think everyone is excited because you get to go home today." I paint on what has been described by the nursing staff as my discharge face. You know, the one that says it was great to have you here, but it's time for you to go. I step around the excited Carter, who is balancing on his skateboard, and approach the bed. Marian takes a deep inhale as I check her vitals. Her pressure is higher than when she arrived yesterday with a broken arm. I check the chart and review the readings from the nurses overnight. Everything else appears in order.

"The nurse has called in your prescription. Drink plenty of fluids, and follow up with your primary care physician in a week." Marion's eyes glaze over as I read my standard discharge statement. Usually, I'd direct any instructions to include the patient's spouse, but I can tell Darin is not that type of partner. "And try not to trip over any more toys at the top of staircases." My attempt at a joke lands flat as Carter's skateboard rolls across the floor again.

I turn when I hear the board stop abruptly. "This is a beauty." Reggie has dropped to one knee and holds the board in front of Carter.

"I got it for my birthday. I'm eight." Carter stands proud.

Reggie twists the board and spins one wheel. "My nephew is ten, and he does all types of crazy stunts with his. Do you know what he told me?"

Little Carter bounces on his toes. "I want to do a kickflip."

"Well, my nephew told me the secret. He said he never rides his skateboard indoors. He goes out to the skate park and the playground. He always wears a helmet and elbow pads. He said once he started doing that, the kids at the playground knew he was responsible enough to learn the real tricks." The room is silent, Carter mesmerized by Reggie's instructions. Even the baby stops whimpering. "You think you can do that?"

Reggie hands the skateboard to Carter, who nods. He slips the board under his arm and begins to squirm due to the weight. Reggie glances at the father and rolls his eyes. He reaches for the skateboard and places it on the father's lap next to the baby.

Reggie turns, and I capture his gaze. This is a side of him I haven't seen before. The caring, empathetic professional. When the corner of his lips ticks up into a smirk, I realize I've been staring for too long.

"Take a picture. It lasts longer," he whispers and steps next to me by the side of Marian's bed.

"Thank you, Doctor..." Marian beams, impressed someone other than her is able to tame her child.

"Dr. Morgan. I was just passing through the floor, and Dr. Carmichael mentioned you to me."

I try not to react, not sure where Reggie is going.

"She asked me to pass this on to you." He hands her the gift certificate to the spa. "Free, compliments of your doctor here. She said you've been an ideal patient and could use a spa day. Isn't that right, Doctor?"

I bite down on my inner cheek and try not to react. He's breaking at least a half dozen rules I can think of off the top of my head, all the while making me a co-conspirator.

"Well." I begin to fumble, not sure how I can walk this back. Thankfully, Marian is not looking at me. She's focusing on the small print of the certificate. The further she reads, the wider her smile grows. That certificate is worth nearly five hundred dollars. "It's not exactly free..."

"Of course not," Reggie says, and I take a breath. "Somebody had to pay for them," he adds, "but not you..." He leans over my shoulder and reads the chart. "Marian. Dr. Carmichael has connections everywhere, and you're all taken care of. Enjoy it—something tells me it's been some time since you've had a spa day."

"Thank you so much. Thank you both," Marian says, clutching the certificate as if it's the best early Christmas gift she's ever received.

I exhale a breath I had been holding. I'll check the hospital policy later. I'm sure if I pay for the certificate, I should be able to get around any violations.

"Please enjoy. And take care of that arm," I state and turn toward her husband, who's back on his phone. "The nurse will be in shortly with the paperwork to discharge you. Be safe out there."

She thanks me again, and I lead Reggie out of the room. He doesn't wait for us to reach the hallway. "You have to admit, we make a damn good team?" he says with that damn sexy smirk on his face. It won't work. The angry smoke from my ears blocks it out.

"Don't ever do anything like that again with my patient." I raise a finger an inch from his face, and it does nothing to remove the smirk.

"Treat the patient, the complete patient," he mutters the mantra of my dad, the statement ingrained in me since I started med school. Visions of the hand-crafted wooden sign in my dad's home office fill my head.

I forget Reggie was mentored by my dad when he performed his residency so long ago. Back when my dad was the respected professional admired by everyone in Rhode Island. Before he decided to play by his own rules.

"It's not always about the medicine," Reggie says, his words echoing my dad's. "Sometimes the best treatment is a smile, a kind word, and the hope of a better tomorrow."

I nod, the fumes of my anger fading. "I know all of this, Dr. Morgan. Marian is my patient, and I was going to treat all of her in my way. Without breaking any rules. You've just cost me five hundred dollars and thirty minutes of paperwork."

His chuckle fills the hallway. "You've got to be kidding. They hand out those certificates like candy on Halloween down in the ER. No one cares, Angie. You don't need to fill out any paperwork. And you certainly don't have to pay for a certificate which the drug company already did."

I stride down the hall toward the elevator but take the detour through the nurses' station. I tap the shoulder of the head nurse on duty, Nurse Chin. "I'm headed to the ER for a consult." She nods and gives a wave to Dr. Morgan; he has fans everywhere.

We reach the elevator, and I pick up our conversation. "I don't know or care to know how things are done in the ER. Here in Ortho and in every part of the hospital I've ever worked, we are given rules and we follow them."

The elevator dings, and we step in. Once the door closes, Reggie leans forward, his shoulder nearly brushing against mine as he presses the button for the ground floor, where the ER is located. His finger lingers over the console as he whispers, "Just remember not all rules are good rules. Don't let a rule stop you from doing what you know is the right thing. Some rules are meant to be broken. Don't be such a stickler."

He reminds me of my reputation. I'm a rule follower, never deviating from what is written in black and white. He may make fun of me, but I don't care. I've seen what happens to those who don't follow the rules. My dad is the poster child. I will not face that same fate.

I ignore Reggie's comment. He's an ER doctor. I work several floors away. We operate in two different worlds, apparently with two different sets of rules.

We descend in silence, Reggie satisfied to have the last word. The doors slide open, and we step into the chaos of the ER, and I brace myself to enter his world.

Chapter Three

The ER is not a foreign place for me. I cut my teeth down here when I began my residency. The hardest and most difficult residency in the hospital according to my dad. The one place he demanded his daughter begin her career. It was stated so often when I was in medical school I interpreted it as a rule. And you already know about me and rules.

Dr. Morgan surprises me by first reporting to the nurses' station. Nurse Reynolds still mans the floor. She's been at this station for nearly a decade, a span that is nearly unheard of in emergency medicine. The stress and burnout rate in the ER is legendary. She, like Dr. Morgan, both having worked with my dad.

She's a no-nonsense old-school nurse, or at least she was when I did my residency. Years of working with my dad and now with Dr. Morgan have moved her to the dark side of accepting doctors bending rules on her watch.

I wait patiently out of the chaos of the nurses' station. The double doors across from the station open and close so frequently they remind me of windshield wipers in a rainstorm. A steady stream of hospital gurneys wielded by exhausted but focused ambulance workers wheel in patients all in dire need of medical attention. It's Friday, and everyone in the hospital is familiar with the pattern. An increase in patients by twenty percent tonight, another ten percent tomorrow night, the hospital's two busiest days for emergency patients.

Eastport General is located in beautiful and relatively quiet Eastport, Rhode Island—small-town America with old factories and new tech startup companies, rural farms, and independent shops. Our uptick in activity at the hospital is all relative. Most of our patients will be from weekend warriors, home repair mishaps, far too many car accidents of people speeding their way to Block Island, and, like most of America, opioid abuse patients.

I press my shoulders back against a cool glass wall and watch in amazement at the synchronicity of the emergency room. Orders are shouted at near pitch volume, the cacophony of machines beeping in their own unique melody, the shouts of patients in distress, the scraping of hospital sneakers across the tiled floors. It's a unique melody not found anywhere else in the hospital, a beautiful symphony heard and appreciated by very few.

I feel the corners of my lips ticking up as I not only recall my time down here, but also visiting my dad on dozens of occasions. He was a true master conductor—that is, until the baton was wretched from his hand.

A blur of white moves quickly in my direction. Dr. Morgan. For some reason, he's graced me yet again with a smug look and a twinkle in his blue-gray eyes. He strides right toward me, the tips of his sneakers tapping mine. "You are the most dangerous thing in the ER. A beautifully intelligent woman who looks like you and smiles like a goddess."

He misinterprets my smile. It has very little to do with him. "I was just smiling in appreciation at the calm of the Ortho floor. And when I think of calm, you are the furthest thought from my mind."

He snickers and waves me to follow. "So you've just admitted you do think of me. I knew my charm would wear you down eventually."

"Yeah, like sulfuric acid mixed with alcohol." The deadly mixture always produces an explosive reaction.

His chuckle is his response, a deep hearty chuckle I'm sure works wonders for him with the first-year residents. Dr. Morgan is a constant flirt. He's been chipping away at me since the day he arrived at Eastport. Eight months of nibbling and scrapping and nothing to show for it. I had expected him to move on after the first thirty days. It's not like he's in want of attention from other staff members. He's practically grown a fan club throughout the hospital.

He hosts not one but two monthly happy hours. One just for the ER staff, no doctors invited, and a second one for doctors. I swear he must have an automated reminder set because, to this day, it arrives in my email box like clockwork. I've yet to attend.

He's a dangerous distraction, and the fact that he was mentored by my dad only makes him even more deadly. If Reggie is like most doctors, they continue to lean on and chat with their mentors even after they've left medicine. Dad has only mentioned Reggie's name to me once, and that was when Dr. Morgan got assigned to Eastport. He told me he's a brilliant physician, and I could learn a great deal from him. That was it, short and to the point, so unlike most of the advice given to me by Dad.

Dr. Morgan sticks his hands under the sanitizer dispenser and rubs them together before walking into the small emergency room. As he scoops up the chart, I take a glob of sanitizer and follow him into the room.

The large kid lifts his head as we enter. Reggie had told me in the elevator the kid is seventeen, but he looks older. African American, curly hair, and hazel eyes. He's going to be a heartbreaker if he's not already. A worried gaze greets us as Reggie steps next to the bed.

"Where is your father?" he asks.

"Just went to the cafeteria for some coffee. He'll be right back." His deep baritone voice surprises me.

"Floyd, this is Dr. Carmichael. She's a specialist in our Orthopedic Unit. I've asked her to join me and check you out." Reggie lifts a hand in my direction as Floyd places weight on his right hand. A grimace spreads across his face.

"That's okay, you don't have to move." I step to the opposite side of the bed, across from Reggie. "How are you feeling? Dr. Morgan says you came in after feeling a pop in your arm?"

A bashful nod floats toward me. "I didn't think it was anything. I was pitching. My dad and I are in town for the baseball tournament." His gaze ping-pongs between Reggie and me. "After I felt the pop, my fastball barely reached eighty miles an hour."

I'm not much of a baseball fan. "And that's not normal?" I ask.

He shakes his head. "Naw, I normally throw ninety-two, ninety-three. I once reached ninety-five. My dad saw the eighty reading and rushed me here in secret."

"In secret?" I ask.

Reggie answers for Floyd. "Floyd has told me he's applied for the baseball draft in a few weeks. Which means he's pretty talented. The last thing he wants the scouts to see is an injury right before the draft."

I nod as Floyd expands, "My dad thinks I have a shot at being drafted by Boston or Milwaukee. If I go first round, there would be a huge signing bonus. So I can't be injured right now."

"We're going to do everything we can to get you back on the field as soon as possible," I add. "Dr. Morgan, what are we looking at?"

Reggie's hand lands on Floyd's right shoulder. "The X-ray shows a hairline fracture in an unusual spot, high in the shoulder near the acromion bone. It should heal on its own in less than a week. We've started him on a drip of acetaminophen to combat the pain and turbocharge the recovery. However, I'd to get your input on what the underlying cause may be. I have a set of X-rays which I can show you over at the nurses' station."

My brow pinches when Reggie mentions the nurses' station. There is a perfectly good display station to the right of the bed. One ER uses all the time when diagnosing a patient. The X-rays are also digitized and available on our iPad. The mention of the nurses' station means Reggie has discovered something disturbing in the X-rays and doesn't want to have the conversation in front of Floyd.

"Of course." I nod in Reggie's direction before pivoting to face Floyd. "We'll be right back and will talk with you and your dad when we return."

I follow Reggie out of the room and we make our way to the nurses' station. He flips his iPad and taps. "Here's his latest X-ray." He pinches the screen and zooms in on the problem area.

I take the iPad from his hand and focus in on the area. The hairline fracture is minuscule and should not be producing enough pain to cripple a healthy teen. My practiced fingers zoom in and out on the various areas around the fracture.

Reggie, for all his bluster, provides me the time and space to analyze the scans. "Where are the results of the BMD test? I suspect..."

"Deterioration, right?" he completes my thought, and I'm reminded again of Reggie's skill. Not many ER doctors would be able to discern this from a simple scan. He leans over my shoulder again, his manly fragrance filling my nose. "I ordered it earlier. Here's the result." He taps a few icons, and the analysis appears.

"These are not the bones of an active teenager." I read the analytical report with the accompanying charts and markers. The numbers don't add up. "And this is the first time he's experienced this pain?"

"First time seeking treatment. He was pitching in a game just last week. Incredible, right?"

"Unbelievable," I mutter. "And all you've found was a hairline fracture in the shoulder? Nothing on the elbow? The wrist? His ankles?"

Reggie taps a few other icons. "I had them shoot the elbow and wrist. They're clean as a whistle. I didn't want to order any for the hip, knees, or ankles because I knew that would lead to a bunch of questions we're not prepared to answer right now."

I nod and scan the X-rays. "You just said *we*. Questions *we're* not prepared to answer."

I twist to take in his reaction. His focus remains on the iPad in my hand as he presses his middle finger to his temple. "Yeah. I'm kind of invested. I didn't want to kick this up to Ortho. We don't get too many cases like this around, and add to it I'd get to work with you... I can't pass up this opportunity. Angie, if you'd have me, I'd like to partner with this together. I want to get this right, and I need your help."

It's the humblest I've ever heard Reggie speak. The fact that he respects me enough to pull me in on what could become a closely watched case here at the hospital hits me in a place none of his thousand flirts have ever reached.

"We'll figure this out." I say the words with a confidence I shouldn't have. With medicine, there are never any guarantees, but for some reason, looking into Reggie's vulnerable eyes, I feel the need to give him the words he needs to hear at this moment. "You've got yourself a partner."

Reggie looks over my shoulder. "Good, his father is back. Let's go speak to them."

I turn in time to spot the back of the tall man entering the room. I follow Reggie through the doorway, both of us scooping a glob of hand sanitizer as we enter.

"Mr. Patterson, welcome back. Let me introduce you to my..." Reggie begins as the man turns to face us.

A familiar set of familiar sexy dark eyes freeze me in place. "Angie...?"

The perplexed, out-of-place face of my one-night stand stares back at me, and there's only one word that escapes my lips. "Brayton?"

Chapter Four

Brayton's brows pinch as he lowers the coffee cup in his hand to his waist. "Angie?" His voice flutters for a second before recovering. "You had mentioned you work in the medical profession. I didn't realize you were a doctor."

I push an errant strand of hair around my ear and avoid his gaze. "Not the only thing we failed to discuss." My gaze travels to his son. I try not to jump to conclusions, and I replay our exchange in the bar. The one deal-breaker question I always ask. I may lower my guard once a month, put on a dress that is more daring than usual, take on a fake name that doesn't fit me, but I never forget to ask this one question. His ring finger is still bare, and I attempt to even out my ragged breathing.

"Umm." Reggie steps to the bed and places his iPad across the metal bar, the clink drawing our attention. "You two know each other?"

"Our paths crossed last evening for a bit," I jump in, afraid of what Brayton may reveal to a colleague who will take in every syllable to be used against me forever. This is the reason why I travel to the other side of town to an out-of-the-way hotel bar. Separation of church and state, and all.

Brayton's shoulders flinch back as if I've assaulted him. I lift a brow and motion with my eyes toward Reggie, but I doubt he picks up on my signal. He places his coffee on the meal tray next to Floyd and takes his son's hand. "Are you here because you have the test results? You said earlier the hairline fracture would heal on its own. Is there more?"

I take a small step back and let Reggie take the lead. I'm the consulting physician, and the rule book states the primary physician should lead any discussions with the patient and the family. "Yes," Reggie begins, "Dr. Carmichael and I have reviewed the latest X-rays. Floyd has a hairline fracture near his right shoulder. It's minuscule, and given his age and overall health, it'll heal on its own within a week. No pitching during this time."

Reggie shifts the iPad behind his back before continuing. "However, we did discover something else that is a little puzzling. Your bone density is not where we would expect it to be. Especially given your age. And it appears to be deteriorating. Is this the first time you've felt pain such as this?"

Floyd's gaze ping-pongs from his dad to Reggie before returning to his dad.

"It's okay, son. Tell them the truth. We're all here to get you back on the mound." Brayton's voice is filled with compassion and support. I suspect he is a good father, even if he failed to mention a son to me last evening. I force myself to focus, pushing away the thought of what other secrets he may have kept from me.

Floyd's chin lowers, his gaze boring a hole into his lap. "It's been about a month or so," he mutters.

"A month?" Brayton reacts before we can. "Why didn't you tell me?"

"We had the playoffs and then the invitational," Floyd says. "The pain only lasted a second or two and then went away. This was the first time my velocity dropped."

The updated information will help us with our investigation. "Did you feel any tingling in your fingertips?" I ask.

Floyd nods. "Just for a split second, right before the pop. Nothing since."

"Do you know what it is?" Brayton looks to me for an answer. I pause and twist my body toward Reggie.

"We need to run some more tests," Reggie chimes in. "With your permission, we'd like to take some blood and tissue samples and search for the cause of the issue."

"Of course, whatever you need to do," Brayton says.

"Will I be able to return to the tournament?" Floyd's eyes fill with a desperation he hadn't displayed up to now.

"Don't you worry about that, son. Let's get you better, and we'll figure out the rest later." Brayton pats his son's leg.

"But Dad? If they find out I'm injured, I won't get drafted. There won't be a signing bonus. We'll lose the house."

I notice Brayton squeeze his son's leg. "Shhh." He shoots a quick glance in my direction before lowering his chin. "We'll talk about it later."

"We'll do our best." Reggie leans in close to the bed, drawing Floyd's attention to him. "You just concentrate on getting better. I'm going to have the nurse come in and draw some blood. We'll also add some vitamins along with the pain meds to your IV to speed up your recovery." He pivots to face me, but not before stealing a quick glance in Brayton's direction. "Dr. Carmichael, may I see you for a moment?"

I merely nod and follow him out of the room. I expect him to turn in the hall to speak, but he continues to stride toward the doctors' lounge in the corner. We're barely two steps in the room when he turns to face me. "Dr. Carmichael, must I remind you of the hospital's rule for dating patients."

His words hit me hard, and I take a step back, my hand landing on the frame of the doorway. I search his face for a smirk or any sign of a joke and come up empty. "Are you freaking kidding me right now? What the hell are you talking about?"

"Please," he puffs out from his cheeks as if my question is ridiculous. "I nearly slipped on the drool coming from Brayton's lower lip. Real smooth with the whole *we just met last evening like two passing ships in the night* thing." Reggie raises his fingers in air-quotes to emphasize his point.

I can't believe the nerve of this man. "How is anything I do in my private life a concern of yours? Besides, it's your patient, not mine, and the patient in question is a seventeen-year-old kid. Or are you insinuating I'm somehow involved with a minor?"

"You are right, the patient is a kid, which means his parent gets to make medical decisions for him. The parent that never took his eyes off of you. The parent who continued to look at you as I provided medical advice as if waiting for you to agree before believing a word out of my mouth. He's into you, Angie, and I don't want that to influence his ability to make the proper decisions for his son, my patient."

I step into the lounge and allow the glass door to close behind me, not wanting anyone in the ER to overhear our conversation. "You came seeking me out, Reggie. You know my reputation. I'm a straight shooter. When I tell you nothing will influence putting the health of the patient first, you shouldn't question it. It's rule number one in the book."

As a woman, I'm used to being challenged on the professional level, but this feels personal. Something I didn't expect from Reggie, of all people. Then I think of all the months of flirtation. I always thought it was a game of his. Is he actually jealous? "Why?"

The word is out of my mouth before I can form a coherent thought. "Why would you even care? I've seen patients, nurses, and other doctors giving you that same look. Your fan club is so large they've incorporated. You are off base, but so what if one man looked at me that way? Why would it be such a terrible thing? You still hold an advantage over me a hundred to one."

His eyelashes flutter as he takes an audible breath, gulping back words, and steps close to me. His eyes lock onto me, and heat rises in my chest. "I'd gladly give up those odds if you'd ever look at me like that just once."

His voice cracks, and I peer at his wanting gaze. They float down toward my lips, and I fear he's about to kiss me in the last place I'd ever want this to happen: in the ER.

I swallow my initial response, not wanting to punish a man who showed a vulnerable side of himself to me for the first time. He truly doesn't know me. I don't share the attraction he harbors, and even if I did, he should know by now I have a rule against dating colleagues.

The door swings open behind me, and we both take a step back. "There you are." I turn to face Brayton; he has one hand on the frame of the door and the other on the doorknob. "I hope I'm not interrupting something."

Reggie gives no quarter. "Of course you were. You are in the doctors' lounge."

"Easy," I whisper and step toward Brayton. "Is Floyd okay?"

He nods. "He's fine. The nurse is with him. I was hoping to talk with you."

I feel Reggie's presence behind me, his words still echoing in my head. "If this is about your son's treatment, Dr. Morgan is the primary physician for your son. You should really..."

Brayton releases the door and raises a hand in my direction. The door slowly closes behind him. "It's not about Floyd." His gaze shoots over my shoulder, and I begin to understand Reggie's concern. "It'll only take a minute," he pleads.

Reggie steps around me, sending a hot stare in Brayton's direction as he walks out of the doctors' lounge without saying a word.

I wait for the door to shut again. "Not here," I whisper. "Let's go upstairs to the Ortho floor. I have an office there."

I don't wait for a response. I know he'll follow. What concerns me isn't answering any medical questions he may have, it's the other questions I know his head must be filled with—the personal ones. The ones I typically avoid by never giving my real name, my phone number, or my place of employment.

Brayton has all three right now, and I know he's looking for even more answers. But so am I.

Chapter Five

We ride up the elevator in silence, my gaze glued to the changing numbers above the door. I count in my head how much longer I can avoid the approaching barrage of questions.

I don't have to look in Brayton's direction. I sense his glare locked on me, willing me to turn and face him. I don't, not with colleagues and patients in the elevator with us. Like the gentleman he is, when the doors open on the sixth floor, he extends his arm for me to lead. I nod, continuing to avoid his dark eyes, and stride directly down the hall. I stop at the nurses' station, where Nurse Reynolds looks up at me, her gaze floating over my shoulder to Brayton.

"I see you brought back goodies from the ER." Her joke lands poorly, and I shoot her my best *be professional* glare.

"The father of the patient I was called for a consult on. I'll be in my office." I don't elaborate any further, knowing it would only lead to more questions.

I tip my head for Brayton to follow, making the mistake of scanning him from head to toe. He's wearing comfortable jeans, a tight three-quarter-length charcoal Henley, and black Puma sneakers. He has a body built for athleisure, and he wears it well.

My office is my sanctuary. At the hospital, I operate on overdrive all day. One hundred percent of my attention and energy is focused on my patients and medicine. I arrive early, stay late, and bury myself in anything that will help a patient or improve my skills as a doctor. My time in my office is spent with quick patient consults, colleague meetings, Zoom meetings with doctors at other hospitals, deep research sessions, and the occasional respite when the tension and pressure get too much.

Like most doctors' offices in the hospital, it's small. There's a two-person couch the length of the entrance wall, a high-top table in one corner with two chairs, and my desk, which is clear of clutter with the exception being the six-by-four picture frame of me and my dad in matching doctor's coats, my first day as a resident. The pride on his face and the joy on mine easily makes it one of my favorite photos and memories ever.

I step around the out-of-place six-foot-tall skeleton that I've been meaning to remove forever. I direct Brayton to the high-top table, but he merely takes a position behind the chair, his hands landing on the back of it. Per habit, upon entering the office, I remove my lab coat and slip it onto the hook on the back of the door, closing it in the process. When I turn, the agitation from Brayton's shoulders has disappeared, his head tilted slightly and the look on his face resembling the look he possessed at the bar last evening.

He inspects me slowly as I approach the table and slip onto the chair. I don't break the spell and feel the heat in the room rise. I'm wearing a comfortable pair of navy dress slacks and a sensible egg-white cotton-blend button blouse—nothing spectacular, but you'd never know that from the look he's giving me.

"You wanted to chat?" I offer up as his eyes snap to mine, not a hint of an apology or his face.

He shakes his head and takes an audible exhale as if breaking out of a trance. "About downstairs..." He stumbles, and I let him. I brace for the questions as I have a few of my own. "Obviously I was thrown by you entering my son's hospital room, but I do have to say a large part of me is relieved."

He catches me by surprise. "Relieved?"

"Yes," he fumbles again. The strong, confident man from last evening is flustered. By me. I'm confused.

His right hand squeezes the back of the chair. "Ever since you left my hotel room his morning, all I've been thinking about is you, Angie." His voice softens. This is not the conversation I thought we were going to have. "I know,

I know." His hand rises for a beat before landing back on the chair. "I know the unwritten rules of a hotel hookup. But it didn't feel like that to me. To be honest, it never did. All day I was racking my brains, checking my social media, hoping you would reach out."

"And then I walked into your son's hospital room." I jettison our conversation to the elephant in the room. "A son you failed to mention. Is there anyone else?" I don't know why I phrase the question the way I do, as if there is a possibility of a future. If he's one of those men who removes a wedding band and lies when he's on the road, I can't expect the truth from him now.

"There is no one, Angie." Gone is the unsteadiness, his voice strong and solid. He finally slips into the chair across from me, his hands palm up on the tabletop, as if expecting me to slip my hands into his. "I didn't lie to you. I didn't mention Floyd because there wasn't any reason to. It wasn't the reason we were both there." His eyes are earnest, and I feel the tension in my body begin to relax. He's either telling the truth, or he's an expert liar. His next sentence clarifies it. "If you go to my socials, you'd see my life. You'd see Floyd everywhere. He's not a secret—he's my life."

He's right. He didn't mention his son, and I didn't ask. He did express interest in more than a one-night stand before I left, directing me to his IG and Facebook accounts. He wasn't trying to hide anything from me. I had thought about it. Briefly, after getting home and getting ready for work, I replayed the evening with him. The easy way we connected, how he seemed to know exactly what I needed every moment of the evening. Even now, he's reading my mind and blocking my objections before I even speak them into the universe.

But my rule stopped me cold.

My focus and energy must be on the job. I have a list of failed relationships over the last decade of men who didn't understand a driven woman, men too insecure to be in a relationship with a doctor, nice men who I gave mixed signals while I figured out what I needed and wanted in life. That's why when I turned thirty, I stepped away from traditional dating, my focus solely on my career. Men were sidelined to an occasional hookup to fulfill my physical desires. Relationships would have to wait. I'm not opposed. Someday, the right man will come along at the right time. But a random hookup in a hotel bar on a weeknight is not the sign I was waiting for. No matter how dreamy he looks or how caring he appears.

I don't speak, merely pulling out my phone and beginning to scroll. "Care to show me yours?" Brayton teases from across the table as he takes out his phone.

My lips squeeze tight, and my head shakes slowly. "I'm not on social media. Hospital policy." I hide behind yet another rule that no one else in the building follows. "I think you've figured out how to contact me." I'm not sure why I float that life raft to a man who appears to have a desperate need to connect. I should feel flattered, but I burned those instincts long ago. The ashes scattered to the four corners of the earth, compliments of too many dreamy-looking men with slippery tongues and truths that didn't stay hidden for long.

My fingers stop scrolling as I digest Brayton's truth. His IG feed is filled with photos of him and Floyd. Baseball games, practices, car drives, and amusement parks. Bike riding and swinging on tubes at lakes. Their matching smiles and joy of life beam across his curated feed that could easily be placed on the Hallmark channel.

I swipe down, seeking his past, seeking his hidden truths. Christmas, birthdays, other gatherings are usually a good giveaway. Yet all I find is him and Floyd. Fellow kids, Floyd's age, mostly baseball teammates based on their outfits, an occasional set of teenaged girls in a group photo. If he's expecting me to relax, I don't. This feed is too perfect, as is the look Brayton is giving me from across the table.

His body is relaxed, shoulders pushed back, a slight prideful smirk on the corner of his lips as he sits patiently waiting for me to react. I offer him a bread crumb. "I have to admit, your selfie game is on point." That hint of a smile blossoms into a full-on dangerous, sexy smile that transports me back to the bar. I blink away the image before changing the conversation.

"What's the link to your other IG account?" The smile falls from his face, and the look of puzzlement that replaces it is nearly as adorable and twice as deadly. "Not the daddy-of-the-year feed you share with all your conquests. Where is the real Brayton Patterson feed?"

I gaze up from my phone, holding it steady, ready to search.

"Sorry to disappoint," he starts, and his eyes flicker to my phone for half a second. "This is me. All of boring me."

As much as I could stare at him all day, the longer this conversation goes, the more questions I will get from Reggie and Nurse Reynolds. Grief I'm not in the mood to deal with today. "Where is Floyd's mom?"

His lips part, his forehead pinches, and he leans forward. "All you need to know for now is she is not in the picture. Hasn't been for a very long time." He pauses, and I wait to see if there is more. "Since we are covering relationships, what is the deal with you and Dr. Morgan? Did I sense some history between the two of you?"

My cheeks puff, and I blow out a ridiculous breath. "I don't mess with colleagues. Another rule of mine."

"It didn't seem like Dr. Morgan agrees with that rule."

"Well, Dr. Morgan has a problem with most rules." I tap the top of the table. "Enough about him. So you are telling me you live the life of a saint? How do you expect me to believe any of that after last night?"

His chuckle fills my tiny office, and I attempt to decipher its meaning. "I never claimed to be a saint. And as for last night, I think it was you who made the first move."

"One that faced zero resistance."

His hand lands next to mine, the skin-to-skin contact of his pinkie finger against mine sending a charge up my arm. I don't move my hand and try to steel the reaction his touch has on me. "I was just a lamb, and you were the beautifully attractive, sexy-as-hell butcher leading me to the slaughter. How could I ever resist?"

I point a finger at his chest and twirl it in his direction. "Does this helpless playboy thing work for most of the girls?"

"Who gives a fuck about most of the girls? Does it work for you?"

He's relentless. The sexy ones I should stay far away from always are. "There is no future here, Brayton. I don't get involved with patients." The excuse sounds as weak in the air as it did in my head.

"I'm not your patient," he counters like the lazy volley it was.

"Your son is, and he's underage, therefore you have medical decision capacity. It's almost the same."

"Almost," he whispers. "I can work with almost." He speaks the words as if directed at himself. "I want to see you again, Angie. I know you must feel what I do. There's something here, and if your life is anything like mine, you know how rare this is."

This is such a bad idea, so why do I hesitate? I've only spent a few hours with him, but I know he's right. Most of my conquests are forgotten before the elevator doors open to the hotel lobby. And if his IG feed reflects even just half of his reality, he is really a caring, kind, gentle soul. I'd be a fool to let this slip away without giving it a chance.

"We live in Springfield, Massachusetts." He attempts to tip the scale, parrying my objections before I voice them again. "One hundred miles from here. An easy drive. A quick train ride and a ridiculously short plane ride." His voice fills with hope, and I picture a younger version of him.

There are so many reasons why I should say no. "Hold on, cowboy. We haven't even been on a proper date, and you have us driving the I-90 shuttle. I barely leave the two-mile radius of the hospital." My statement echoes back at me, my pathetic truth bared to a man who is making it a habit of extracting it from me.

My life is centered around the hospital. My apartment is within walking distance. Every venue, with the exception being the hotel, is safely within a two-mile distance. My cocoon protects me, delivers normalcy, consistency, safety. Yet, it took a venture outside the radius to cross paths with an intriguing man, something I've not found in a long time. Maybe it's time I expand my horizons.

He places the palm of his hand on the back of mine, the electrical spark undeniable. I lift my gaze from our hands to capture his desirous look locked on me. "Okay, let's take it one step at a time. It looks like Floyd is staying the night at the hospital. Visiting hours end at 8:00 p.m. I can meet you in the hospital lobby, and we can go out on a proper date."

I bite my lower lip, failing to suppress the grin forming just below it. How is it possible that just the thought of going on a real date has my chest thumping with excitement? Am I that pathetic?

"And since you never leave the immediate area, I will do the research and find us a perfect spot that is at least three miles away from the hospital." He runs a finger up my forearm, stopping just below my bicep. The small movement causes my smile to fade, my lips to part, and my breath to hitch. He's building a road map to our evening, letting me know what waits for us at the end of the date.

"You are going to have me breaking all my rules," I whisper to myself, but when his brow quirks up, matching the victorious half grin, I realize I've spoken too loud.

He takes my hand and lifts it, placing a soft, warm kiss on the back of my hand. "I'll see you at eight."

I don't rise, afraid that my legs won't cooperate. I don't even turn, waiting for the sound of the door closing. When it does, I release the breath I'd been holding since he kissed my hand. "Holy guacamole!"

Angie Carmichael, the doctor who is married to her job, has a freaking date.

Chapter Six

The number of times I checked the clock during my shift should have been the first clue that I still hadn't recovered from Brayton's sudden appearance at the hospital. Most days, my focus is so intense that the only indication the day is over is when the nursing staff changes. Not today.

When Nurse Chin waves good night to me, I nearly bowl her over hustling back to my office. Reggie pinged me an hour ago to swing by his office at the end of the shift to review Floyd's test results. I still have two hours until I have to meet Brayton in the lobby, yet it doesn't feel like I have enough time to prepare. I've not felt this excited since the season finale of *Grey's Anatomy*, the show every doctor derides to their colleagues but secretly watches every week.

I lock the office door and decide to change outfits now, unsure how much time Reggie will need to discuss the test results. I keep a few outfits in my office. Some to cover the occupational hazards that come with being a doctor, the spattered blood, vomit, etc. The other outfits are for the out-of-nowhere coverage invitations from the administration to join a high-level meeting or to fill in last minute at a donor event or fundraiser. It's from the corner of the closet of the latter that I pull my olive silk top and black pencil skirt. A sensible pair of black pumps complete the ensemble. I adjust my hair and touch up my makeup and slip my lab coat back on, covering my outfit. I grab my emergency overnight pouch, the one I use for the all-nighters that come with the job or when I need to touch up before an event. The small pouch holds a toothbrush, toothpaste, mouth wash, deodorant, and a small bottle of perfume. I lay it next to my pumps, slipping back into my tennis shoes, hoping that will be enough to keep Reggie from an inquisition.

As I make my way to the elevator, iPad tucked underneath my arm, I replay the encounter with Brayton and Reggie's reaction. Reggie has never explicitly asked me out on a date in the eight months he's been at Eastport General. However, I've made it clear on numerous occasions my rule against dating colleagues. This hasn't prevented him from a deluge of flirtatious remarks, sideways glances, and sexy smirks being delivered on a regular basis.

That's all I ever thought they were, Reggie being Reggie. However, the green streak he showed earlier has me questioning this assessment. I'm hoping we can quickly get past it and concentrate on our patient. Something Reggie said did hit home for me. He's been looking forward to working with me. That's all I wish for from all the senior colleagues in the hospital. For them to see me as a valued professional they can work with whenever they face a crisis or challenge. It's why I work so hard, why I have so many rules, why I try to separate my work life from my social one.

It only takes me two minutes to reach Reggie's office on the administrative ninth floor. I knock softly on the frame of his door with my phone in hand. I linger as he turns his attention from his iPad to me, the wide-eyed gaze and momentary jolt of his head as he spots my bare leg peeking out from lab coat—the secret of my outfit beneath the lab coat exposed in under three seconds.

His gaze performs a long, seductive perusal over me. The stare is so intense I can practically feel it hovering over every inch of my skin. "I didn't realize our consult was a formal affair," he teases, floating the statement with a half smirk, pausing for my reaction.

He's seated on the couch, one that is nearly twice the size of mine. He lowers his iPad to the coffee table in front of the couch, his hand patting the large empty space next to him.

I make note he's not wearing his white hospital lab coat. Very few doctors do once they are in their office. I slip down to the couch as my gaze spots the tall bookcase in the corner filled with medical journals and reference books.

The case reminds me of my dad and his preference for touching and skimming hardcover books even after the digital revolution.

"An event later this evening," I mutter, hoping to skip past my plans and focus on the consultation.

"So much for my idea of making this a working dinner meeting." He lowers his chin but not before I see the hint of disappointment sweep across his face. He scoops up his iPad. "The first set of test results came in a half hour ago." He twists the iPad and hands it to me. I appreciate that he doesn't mansplain the information, choosing to sit quietly and allow me to process it and draw my own conclusions. This is the side of him I appreciate, a side of him he doesn't show often.

I feel my brow pinch as I tap the chart and drill into the readings and numbers. I form a quick opinion myself before flipping to the technician's notes and the formal results in the preliminary report.

"So, no cancer?" I say, relieved, knowing Reggie had to have reached the same conclusion. It was the unspoken hypothesis we both formed the minute we saw the bone deterioration. The C word, however, carries with it massive emotional weight, and therefore doctors rarely speculate with the family until they have better information.

"The family will be relieved. However..." Reggie starts, and I already know where he's headed.

"There's nothing definitive to explain the erosion of bone density. We have a medical mystery." Mysteries take time to solve. I force myself to stay in the moment, knowing I have a ticking clock in the back of my head. "Could it be Levinson's syndrome?"

"His triglycines levels rule that out," Reggie counters immediately, displaying once again his deep knowledge in this area. "His respiration rate rules out Barkin's disease, and the fact that he can walk eliminates muscular mypodolopedia."

My focus returns to the charts, and I continue to eliminate other possible causes. For the next hour, we bounce suggestions off one another, eliminating each for one reason or another. It's a beautiful groove, like two jazz players on stage in synch with one another, one starting a melody, the other finishing. The back-and-forth has a familiar feel to it. I recall my dad drilling me with his cases from the ER, challenging me to perform diagnoses while I was studying in med school. I knew a lot less then, but he treated me like an equal, guiding me toward investigative paths rather than telling me an answer. If I ever got stumped, he'll tell me to sleep on it, and the next morning, I'd find a yellow index card on the top of my dresser with the answer.

I pause and take a deep breath. Reggie is sitting behind his desk, head down, staring at a reference book while his fingers hover over the keyboard of his laptop. I have three other reference books laid out in front of me on the coffee table. My lab coat is laid across the back of Reggie's office chair. I don't even recall taking it off. I'm surprised Reggie didn't mention my outfit.

Between the two of us, we've eliminated over two dozen possible causes and have only identified two possibilities, which will require additional research. My phone vibrates across the coffee table, startling both of us. My calendar reminder to meet Brayton. I silence it but not before Reggie catches my sheepish expression.

"What was the alarm for?" he asks, and his eyes widen as he notices my outfit for the first time. "Right, you have an event. If it's one of the hospital cocktail parties, I can join you, and we can continue our discussion." I'm not sure if him seeking an invitation is professional curiosity to continue what has been a surprisingly good working session or a personal query from his green counterpart.

I begin to close the reference books. "Not that type of event. We can pick up the research tomorrow." I float the offer, hoping to deflect him from me leaving. I stand, picking up one of the books, and take a step toward his bookcase.

"You can leave the books. I think I'll keep at it for a bit." He rises from his chair, his gaze slowly raking over me like earlier. "I guess the gossip mill has you incorrectly pegged."

I shouldn't fall for the bait, but I do. "How so?"

"All this time, I was told you were married to your work. I was halfway hoping to pull an all-nighter with you." I expect the words to be filled with something they are not. "Your exploits are near legendary. You lead the entire Ortho department in double shifts and hours. You live a few blocks from the hospital." There is no condensation or condemnation in his tone; if anything, it is filled with pride.

"I do have to admit to being a little conflicted," he continues. "I don't know whether to be jealous of the man who got you interested in something other than the hospital or thank him for delivering you to my office looking the way you do."

He tips his head to the side, an eager look on his face, one filled with hope I'll fill in the blanks for him.

I won't. "I enjoyed this working session."

He twists his hands by his waist, palms up. "Should I even bother to ask?"

"Good night, Dr. Morgan. I'll see you tomorrow."

He points his index finger in my direction, a smirk on his face. "Have a pleasant evening, Angie. Don't break any rules tonight."

My small head shake is my only response. I lay the lab coat across my arm and close his office door behind me.

I have just enough time to drop the coat back in my office, switch out to my pumps, touch up my hair and makeup, and meet Brayton down in the lobby. Reggie's words echo in my head as I enter the empty elevator.

I've not gone on a date in so long, it certainly feels as if I'm breaking a rule.

Chapter Seven

E astport General's lobby is stunning. I make it a point to enter through the main lobby every day to steal a glimpse at the thirty-foot ceilings, the multicolored glass chandelier, the white-and-gray marble floor, and the rows of golden plaques of all the doctors that have left a mark in this community.

Pride fills my chest each time I peruse the line of distinguished physicians, and every single time, my heart breaks when I pause at the one empty spot on the symmetrically aligned grid. The only plaque ever removed in the hospital's nearly century-long history—my father's.

Movement out of the corner of my eye causes me to react. Brayton pops up from a couch to the left, his phone stuffed into a black-and-gold blazer jacket. A small smile pulls on the corner of my lips, surprised that in the middle of caring for his son, he found time to change for our date.

That damn sexy gaze of his rolls over me. Even from the distance of a few feet, I feel it. A tingle racing up my legs, through my core, a foreign warmth through my chest until it settles on my widening grin.

Damn, this man is gorgeous. A simple but Brayton-perfect gold turtleneck grips his defined chest, a thin gold chain lying across it. Black dress slacks and black leather shoes complete his simple but elegant outfit, and he answers the question of whether he can wear an outfit other than athleisure just as well. He can.

A twinkle in his eye makes me feel incredibly special as I step to him, and he pulls me into a hug. His smooth cheek presses against mine, and I take in the woodsy fragrance of his cologne. "Did you shave for me?" Of all the things to ask, it's the first thing that pops in my head, causing a giggle to escape my lips, loud enough to float up to the thirty-foot ceiling.

"Showered too," he jokes and leans back. Our hands remain intertwined, and we take a few beats and smile at each other like silly teenagers. This is a foreign feeling for me, and the fact that I'm doing all this in the lobby of my place of employment reveals more to me than I care to admit. He releases one hand and turns back toward the table in front of the lobby couch. I spot the bouquet. I recognize the wrapping—it's from the hospital gift shop. "If you were impressed I showered and shaved, you're going to love this."

He hands me the bouquet, and I press it to my chest. "I guess this officially makes it a date." It's not the fanciest bouquet I've ever received, and the fact that it came from the hospital gift shop definitely limited his choices, but it truly is the thought that counts. I tip up on my toes and plant a soft kiss on his lips. Last evening, we shared dozens of kisses, all of them ten times more intense than this one, yet my shoulders shudder because this isn't a kiss between strangers who don't expect to see each other again. This kiss is a *we're going on a date and this could be the start of something* kiss. It's chaste, it's quick, but it's public and holds more weight than any of our other kisses.

"You look gorgeous," he whispers, and his gaze lowers. I pause and let him take in my outfit, pleased when his satisfied eyes return to mine. He quirks his chin toward the hospital exit. "My car is out this way."

I motion for him to lead the way, needing a second to catch my breath. It's been less than two minutes, yet I feel the ground shift beneath my feet. This night holds the potential to turn my world upside down, and I remind myself he's just a man. There have been others that struck my interest, who have charmed me, that got my hopes up to only to turn into a pumpkin. As he pushes through the door, I mutter to myself, "It's just a dinner. Just a dinner."

***

Care and thought are put into his restaurant selection, another reflection of a man who I must take a closer look at. Unlike most men, the more I see, the further intrigued I become. The restaurant is a true farm-to-table rustic-modern American restaurant on the edge of town, sitting on the border of Joe Miller's farm. His daughter, Daphne, grew up on the farm, went to culinary school, and returned. She and her father built this restaurant from scratch.

It is known for its healthy, fresh, simple dishes and a menu that changes with the seasons. Many of my colleagues at the hospital rave about this place, yet this is my first time here.

I spear a roasted carrot on the end of my fork and tip it in Brayton's direction. "Tell me again how you found this place. They don't advertise, and it's well off the beaten path."

Brayton's blazer hangs on the back of his chair, his tight turtleneck distracting me in the best of possible ways. He leans forward, a comfortable smile forming, "When Floyd took a nap and I snuck out to the gift shop for the flowers, I asked the manager; this is one of the places she listed. I called the concierge back at the hotel, got a list from him. Talked to three or four nurses and then consulted with Google. This was the one place on everyone's list."

I can't help but return his glowing smile. He made a perfect choice. Our table is on the second-floor terrace, facing out to a set of floor-to-ceiling windows overlooking the darkened farm. This far from town, the twinkling stars in the clear sky light up the empty field. It is so Rhode Island and so perfect.

"Dr. Morgan stopped by just before visiting hours ended." Brayton's fork tings when he rests it against the plate, his hand pressed palm down next to it on the white tablecloth. "He said you have ruled out a number of possible causes for his condition..." He clears his throat. "Including cancer."

My left hand sweeps across the table and lands on the top of his. His gaze lowers from mine to the flickering candle. I've seen this look a hundred times; just the mention of the word "cancer" is enough to flip a family's life upside down.

He tilts his head for a moment before continuing. "I hadn't realized it was a possibility. We didn't realize how serious this has become. What do you think it might be?"

My breath catches as I beat back my instinct to speak. Reggie is the primary physician, and I need to maintain a clear distinction for Brayton. "Dr. Morgan and I won't stop until we figure it out," I start, pulling my hand back slowly.

"He's a good kid," Brayton mumbles. "Why is this happening? And why now of all times?" It's a rhetorical question, but I dive in any way.

"What do you mean, why now?"

He pulls his hands from the top of the table, stuffing them onto his lap, his gaze avoiding mine. "I mean... everything we've worked for over the last six years." He finally dares a look in my direction, a strange look sweeping across his face. He must read my confusion. "The baseball draft next month?"

I'm not much of a sports fan, especially kid sports, and it must be written on my face.

"For the last six years, Floyd has followed his dream to become a professional Baseball player." The flame from the candle flickers off his softened gaze as his voice fills with a tenderness that is a parent's love. "He had outgrown the local Little League in Springfield by the time he was ten years old. So, I signed him up for travel baseball, the top athletes for their age group from across the city. When he quickly proved one of the best there, we moved up to state travel baseball teams. He started playing against kids two and three years his senior. He was only thirteen when the first scout approached us. I'll never forget that day or the look on Floyd's face. The day someone other than his dad told him he was special.

"From that day forward, I knew I would do everything in my power to allow him to chase his dream."

As Brayton takes a sip of his wine, I allow his words to marinate. Pieces of the puzzle are coming together. The reason why he is in Eastport so far from home for a baseball tournament. Floyd's frustrated response in the hospital room about their financial condition. "Travel baseball must be expensive," I probe.

His eyelashes flash as he shakes his head. "You have no idea. The equipment, the personal coaches, time spent at the batting cage, team events, let alone the traveling, hotels, and meals on the road."

"Well, dinner is on me," I offer and prepare for the rebuke from a prideful man.

He raises a hand. "No. That's not what I meant. This is a date." I feel the sincerity in his voice and back down.

"Okay." A wave of silence floats across our table as Brayton glances out at the field. "Hey, does his mom help out?" It's a question that has been nagging in the back of my head since I discovered he has a seventeen-year-old son.

He lowers his chin but not before I spot the grimace pull on his face.

"Sore subject? We don't have..."

"No." His soft response halts me. "If we're going to have a future, I want you to know."

A future.

Brayton reminds me again of his intentions with me. It's not a line used by a traveling man looking to score. It's an unguarded, unplanned, honest reply that has my heart tapping away. He's sincere.

"Floyd's mother, Erin, and I dated in high school. We were young and foolish and got pregnant senior year. Both our families were disappointed, but her family took it to a whole other level. They told her they wouldn't help out with the unborn child, that she needed to figure things out on her own."

"Wow," I mutter, attempting to understand how people that claimed to love you could do something so horrible in a time of need.

"After hearing Erin's situation, my parents offered to take her in. My mom even offered to help raise our kid so we both could go to college. I wouldn't allow them to do that." Brayton chews on the inside of his cheek, and I sense their story is about to take another turn.

"I knew how much Erin had always dreamed about being a fashion designer. So I worked out an agreement with her. I'd stay home, raise Floyd while she'd go off to college. Once she graduated, it would be my turn."

I bite my lower lip, already sensing what came next.

Brayton twists, his gaze floating out the window toward the dark field, his face etched in a painful memory. "Her school was in New York, yet she barely made it home on any breaks. Her sophomore year, she met someone else. A foreign student from France. She claimed it was real love and broke up with me. Floyd was the only possible reason keeping her here, but it wasn't enough. By junior year, she cut off all contact, and after graduation, she moved to France with her boyfriend."

"How could—" I catch myself too late. What a shitty way to break up with someone who was sacrificing for them. How could a mother leave their child?

Brayton's snicker catches me by surprise. "It was actually for the best." A half smirk pulls across his face, and I don't get a single trace of anger or regret from him. "My parents made her sign off on any legal rights to Floyd once we realized she was not coming back. I was working construction, made enough to move from my parents' place, and it's been Floyd and me ever since."

"I'm so sorry..." My blood is boiling. Floyd's mother broke the number rule of parenting: love your child.

I feel Brayton's hand underneath the table squeeze my knee. "That's why I say he's my life. Because he always has been—always will be."

"And the draft next month?" I circle back to where we began.

A bright smile rips across his face once again, the love he has for his child unquestionable. "Floyd is one of the top twenty high school players in the country. He's poised to go in the first round of the draft. Typically, a first-round pick gets a seven-figure signing bonus."

A million-dollar bonus to a seventeen-year-old? I chose the wrong profession.

Now I get it. The draft is their lottery. Their one chance to climb up from a life of sacrifices. An opportunity to get ahead in life.

It's my turn to chew on the inside of my cheek. I'm already connecting the dots, finally understanding his earlier statement about timing. My back stiffens as time is no longer a luxury Reggie and I can afford. I understand the dilemma even before Brayton spells it out to me.

Brayton states the obvious, removing his hand from my knee. "They don't draft injured ballplayers."

Chapter Eight

B rayton's words continue to echo in my brain an hour later. A sense of urgency floods my veins, the need to solve Floyd's medical mystery even greater. Brayton winds his car around a pickup truck and signals off the main road. It's not just Floyd's life that is in the palm of my hand but in many ways his too.

At the bar last evening, Brayton mentioned he's a remote salesman for a materials supply company, working closely with construction companies. I get the sense the salesman job pays less than his former construction job, but it provides him the flexibility to work from the road and travel with his son. Yet another sacrifice he makes. Floyd's mention of the second mortgage on their home reminds of how tight things must truly be.

"This isn't the way back to town," I mention as the road shifts to a winding single-lane country road. Brayton slows and flicks his high beams on. He pinches his eyes tight in concentration.

"I thought it too early to call it an evening. Something tells me you need a long night out nearly as much as I do."

He is right. Most nights, I would be curled up on my couch with a medical journal in one hand and a patient's chart in another. I lean back into the seat and enjoy the quiet. Just being driven by someone else feels like a treat. Another simple pleasure I hadn't realized I had been missing.

I twist the knob on the radio and turn up the music, which had been streaming in the background. The soft, soulful sound causes me to rock my shoulders. "I know this song."

A sexy chuckle fills the car cabin. "Not this version."

He's right. I begin to whisper the words. "Love is a battlefield. I never heard it like this. Who's singing?"

Headlights of a passing car light up the cabin, and I catch a flash of his bright, beautiful smile. It's nice to see him relaxed after a tension-filled day spent at the hospital. "That's my girl Maysa. One of few artists who can take an original and improve upon it." He steals a quick glance in my direction before ricocheting his attention back to the road. "Girl bends every rule to her will and creates something new, something better. It takes a special person to do something like that. Press number four on the CD player."

I do as instructed, and another familiar tune floats through the car. "She redid a Justin Bieber hit..."

The artist has somehow taken a sensual anthem and made it even more erotic. "As long as you love me," I spurt out the title of the song, and I snap my fingers.

He twists toward me, his right-hand landing on my knee, his other remaining on the wheel. I turn to capture his gaze locked on me. His gravely baritone voice grunts the title of the song in a whisper that feels as if his lips are pressed to my ear. A sliver of his tongue peeks out, and my mouth goes dry. The remake is a slow, sexy tempo made for grinding against a wall in a darkened room. Images of Brayton and me underneath his hotel sheets, bodies sweating, moving at a rhythm fill my head and cause me to squirm in my seat.

"Can you do me a favor?" he asks totally aware of what his words are doing to me.

My breath hitches, "Anything." The word slips out sounding as desperate as I feel.

The glint in his eye confirms its receipt. His wink causes me to bite down on my lower lip. "Can you repeat the name of the song for me." The command comes across like a plea of a man who has faced struggles and needs to be reminded that despite the mountains in front of him, there is a prize waiting on the other side.

I twist in my seat to face him and allow a beat to pass as I gather myself. "As long as I love you," I state the title of the tune without a hesitation, without overthinking the moment.

Brayton's gaze returns to the road, a nod of satisfaction the corners of his lips ticking up slightly. The hum of the road comforts us as Brayton's hand returns to the wheel as he twists around a bend. Maysa continues singing her anthem to love. Her bold rendition reminds us that even with the joy of love, there is pain and sacrifice. That nothing else matters when love is a possibility. No challenge too big, no road too difficult to travel, as long as you have love.

Of all the songs for him to ask me to press Play on, of all the messages he wants me to hear tonight, this is the one he chooses. The one that has a permanent place on his player. A song about love and sacrifice.

This is his heart song.

I get lost in the words as a peaceful silence falls between us. I'm just a woman lost in the confusion of navigating a demanding profession, and he's just a man dropping his guard and sharing with me what he is looking for.

"There we are..." he says, and I twist in time to see the lights ahead.

A country bar well off the beaten path. The small billboard lists it at the Wildhorse Saloon. Brayton steers the car through the dirt parking lot in between two pickup trucks, one sporting a confederate flag. My fingers form a fist in the seat, my body on alert, my mood shifting from pleasure to danger in a heartbeat. "I'm not sure this is the type of bar you may think..." I caution.

Rhode Island may technically reside in the north, but like most of America, there are strong elements of racism no matter where you go. I fear Brayton may not be aware.

"Trust me, it's exactly what I think it is," he returns with a confidence I hadn't expected.

"Have you been here before?"

"Never ever heard of it until a few hours ago." He cuts the engine and kills the lights, clicking open the door.

"Hold up," I say, reengaging the locks. "You do realize we are black, right?" It's the only thing I can think to say that will snap him out of the bubble he must be living in right now. "You did see the flag on the truck you pulled in next to? They might as well roll out a sign that says 'not welcome'." I may sound dramatic, but I'm not. We are out in the middle of nowhere at a saloon neither one of us has ever been, and no one on the planet knows where we are. A chill races through my veins. If this scene played out on a movie screen, I'd be the one yelling the loudest, *"Take off those shoes, girl, and run."*

Brayton unlocks the doors again and juts his chin toward the bar. Three white men in their mid-forties stand outside the bar sipping beers. Two are wearing cowboy hats. "Do you see that American flag at the door?"

It takes me a long shaky breath to probe the hips of the men on the porch. I expect to see leather holsters and open-carry firearms. I exhale when all I make out are worn leather belts from Sam's Club. Behind them on both sides of the doorway underneath the lights swinging in the breeze are two large American flags.

"When I see that, I see the possibilities of the country I love," Brayton says wistfully, and I turn to see if he has his hand over his heart, about to recite the Pledge of Allegiance.

My hand lands on his forearm. "When I see it, I see the hard road we've traveled in this country, the history and the heartache."

He lays his free hand on top of my cold and clammy one. "Do you trust me?"

It's a funny question because none of my concerns about this situation involve him. "I didn't bring my medical bag, Brayton, and I charge extra if I have to use thread and needle to stitch you up." I attempt to lighten the mood but also make him aware of my concerns.

"Good to know. Let's go." Before I can take another breath, he's outside my car door, helping me out. He hooks his arm, and I hesitate. I can't read his face in the darkness of the parking lot, but when he pokes my side with his elbow a second time, I slip my hand through, holding him tighter than anytime outside of his hotel room.

I lower my chin to avoid the gaze of the men as we approach the saloon. One of the men steps to the side and holds open the door. "Evening, gents," Brayton says, and I feel like I'm sitting on my childhood couch watching a western with my dad. Any second, I expect a cheap wooden chair to be broken across our backs and a body to come flying through the glass window.

"Evening, ma'am." I look up in time to see the men tip their hats in my direction. I search their faces and am met with small genuine smiles.

"Evening," I whisper and follow Brayton into the saloon.

Warm light wood greets us, along with three rows of Edison lights hanging from a high ceiling. A large L-shaped bar frames two sides of the room, each section running nearly fifty-feet long. Bar stools and two-person high-top tables run the length of the bar, but the draw of the room and the true reason Brayton selected this bar resides in the center of the room.

Two steps down is a massive sunken dance floor. Nearly three dozen people dot the floor, all moving in synchronization. "Cotton Eye Joe" blares from the overhead speakers as two women and one man stand in front of the crowd and shout out dance instructions.

"You country line dance?" I fail at hiding the surprise in my voice.

His hand slips around mine, and he leads me down the steps. "I have layers. I pray you stick around and remove them all." He places a quick peck on the top of my head before stopping next to two blonde women in their thirties. Quick, short smiles from the two of them ease my concern. I'm not surprised we are the only two people of color in the room.

"Just listen for the instructions and follow the people around you. The dance has a short step sequence which is repeated over and over. I know you'll pick it up quickly." Brayton's confidence in me lowers my remaining concerns.

It takes me only about thirty seconds to figure out the sequence. Brayton is already an expert. He points and shouts out the steps, and I picture him on the baseball field with an eleven-year-old Floyd. Watching the patience and joy Brayton has in teaching, it's no wonder Floyd fell in love with baseball. Never in a million years would I have thought I'd go country line dancing. Within three songs, I already know it's something I'll never tire of.

The dance floor is filled with people of all shapes and ages. Girlfriends hanging together, young couples, and old married couples. Every one of them is laughing and enjoying themselves. The next song involves partner moves, and Brayton hooks an arm across my shoulder and leads me. He whispers instructions to me and focuses down on my footwork. Even from here, I can see he's simplified the steps for me as people around us perform a more elaborate version.

After I pick up the step, he gives me another quick kiss on my temple. His heated breath has my mind racing to places not normally associated with a first date. This really is a first date. "I knew from the way you moved last evening you'd pick this up quickly."

Heat fills my cheek, a blush forming as my head fills with images of the moves he must be visualizing.

"As you can see, this is more than just a bar. I hope you don't mind," he whispers and waits for my reaction. His hands slide slowly down from my shoulders to my hips.

"Not at all. I can tell from your moves this isn't your first rodeo."

"Cowboy humor. I like it." He pulls me tight against his chest and laughs. The humor drops from his voice when he starts up again. "Floyd's tournaments take us all across America. Most evenings, the kids want to hang out together, and the few parents are left to their own devices. I quickly tired of the dinners and bar scene where the rich parents talk about stock options and conquering the world. I've always been a fan of music, and after sitting in a baseball stadium all day, I needed to move."

I push off his chest and lean my head back to capture every word.

"One thing America has plenty of, no matter how small the city is, are bars. And the further the games got from big cities, the more often my paths crossed with country line dance bars. I understand your hesitation in the parking lot. That was me the first time I went. I brought along four of the white parents with me so they could run interference, just in case. It wasn't necessary. These bars are really filled with good people just like us looking to relax and enjoy some music. I've been in over thirty states and haven't had an issue inside a bar."

I nod and give him a pass on his implication. If only the spirit shared on the dance floor would seep outside the doors of every saloon in America. Story for another day.

Somewhere along the conversation, we'd fallen out of step with the dance. We are merely swaying to the music. I glance over Brayton's shoulder to see if anyone notices. The blonde woman next to me captures my gaze, and she winks at me with a smile.

I return the smile and turn my attention back to Brayton. I run my hand from his shoulder to the back of his neck, giving it a slight pull. He leans down, and I press my lips to his. His kiss is warm, it is sweet, it is perfect. "Let me buy my sweet man a drink," I whisper and take his hands, leading him off the dance floor.

Three minutes later, we sit at a high-top, staring down at the dance floor. The instructional hour has ended, and the tempo and level of complexity of the dances have increased. "Looks like we got off the dance floor just in time," I joke.

"Nothing you couldn't handle. Just like in life," Brayton returns. On most guys, these words would roll off my shoulders as a pickup line, but with him, they hit hard.

I step around the table to reward him, my lips on his again. I taste the lime from his drink on his breath. This kiss is the sweetest thing I've tasted in a long time. Soft, tender with a passion I'm learning he brings to everything. His fingers thread through my hair as he cups me by the back of my head, and our kisses intensify. I can barely breathe, I can barely think, yet all I want is more.

I clear my throat to make sure I'm heard on the first try, knowing I won't have the courage to repeat myself. "My dance card is all yours – nothing on the calendar until I report to work in the morning."

Brayton's hand freezes, and my heart stops, fear racing through my body that I've read this situation wrong. His gaze softens, yet the desirous flame continues to burn in his eyes. "Are you sure? This is technically a first date. We don't..."

I cut him off. "I wouldn't have said what I said if I wasn't."

He places a ghost kiss on my lips before speaking. "Do you want another dance before we go?"

I shake my head. This evening was supposed to douse whatever it was I thought existed between us. A few hours not in his bed should have been the dose of reality that would cool both of us off from thinking we might have a future together. Instead, it's done the opposite. "I want to see your moves, Brayton, but not the ones on the dance floor. Let's go back to your hotel room."

I embrace the feelings developing between us. He is a good man; I repeat it to myself over and over again, not giving space to any of the voices in my head to remind me of the half-dozen rules I have to protect myself from doing exactly what I'm about to do.

He's a good man, he's a good man. He has to be.

Chapter Nine

W e ride in a comfortable silence up the hotel elevator. It's twenty-four hours since we last took a similar ride, this one so different. This time I'm not in the corner of the elevator attempting to hide my nervousness, hyperaware of every move the strange man I had persuaded to take back to his room made.

This time my heartbeat is steady, my nerves calm, a sense of joy racing through my veins and a look of admiration on my face. Brayton continues to be a pleasant surprise in all the right ways.

On the slow, windy road back to the hotel, he told me stories of Floyd growing up. The thousand missteps he made as a young, inexperienced single parent. The pledge he has made and has kept that Floyd never misses out on any opportunity because of his home situation. He could be the poster child for single dads around the world. Every action, every decision he makes is centered around Floyd's needs.

This man sacrifices daily and never once looks to be taken care of himself. It's an attractive trait that has me thinking of ways I can ease his burden. I wish I had raced home and properly packed an overnight bag with the silk lingerie I haven't worn in forever. I'll have to improvise.

He swipes the hotel card and holds the door open for me to enter. The curtains are open, and I step toward the window as he clicks on the lights. As he hangs his sports jacket in the closet, I take in the room. We never turned on the lights in the main room last night, and now I can see things I had no clue of last evening.

The travel baseball pamphlet and schedule on the coffee table, the sports duffel bag with two aluminum bats sticking out the bottom of the closet by the door. A baseball glove with a worn baseball inside sitting on the couch near the window.

Brayton notices my gaze and strides toward the couch scooping up the glove. I take advantage of his distraction and swipe the collared shirt hanging in his closet. I pull it off the hanger and fold it behind my back. "I'm gonna get comfortable," I whisper to him as I press my lips to his. The warm, sweet kiss is expected and cherished. I slip the strap of my bag over my shoulder. "Be ready when I get out." I wink at him and disappear into the bathroom.

It's been a long while since I've not slept with a stranger, and I had forgotten how nice it feels. I don't have to overthink. The reflection of a happy woman stares back at me in the mirror, and I blow it a kiss. I take my time changing into the huge white shirt that hangs down to my knees. I roll the sleeves up past my elbows and only secure the shirt with one button. My modest bosom threatens to peek out as I twist side to side in the mirror – the perfect amount of tease. I imagine Brayton on the other side of the door stripping down to his tight boxers, the anticipation building to a crescendo. I take one final glance in the mirror and take a long inhale. A quick pep talk flashes through my head—*you can do this, you deserve happiness, he's a good man.*

I crack open the door, my tongue swiping across my lower lip. "Are you ready for me?"

"More than you'd ever know," he returns, and I giggle.

I push open the door but only allow my left leg to kick out. The movement causes the tail of the shirt to ride up my leg my shapely, brown leg.

"Oh my." I hear the deep chuckle from across the room, and I picture him standing in front of the couch.

"Ladies and gentlemen, may I present to you..." I tease and strut out of the bathroom, hands raised to the ceiling, hips swaying side to side. "What the hell?" My brows pinch with confusion as I spot a fully clothed Brayton in front of the very much pulled-out couch, a pillow and blanket underneath his arm. "What's going on?"

He steps to me and places a kiss on the top of my head. "You look beautiful." His words do not match his actions.

"Why is the pull-out couch... out?"

"Hear me out first." He adjusts the pillow to in front of his body, both hands crossed against it. "I had a great evening, Angie. One of the best I can ever recall."

I pull the collar of the shirt tight against me, unsure of what the hell is going on.

"And as much as I'd like for it to continue... I do have a request."

My eyes scan over his shoulder and into the corners of the room, looking to see if I missed something. "What type of request?"

He turns back toward the couch and drops the pillow and blanket. "I think we can have something special between us. I hope you feel it."

Two minutes ago, I would have agreed without thinking. His actions, however, have me frozen in place.

"I do," he continues. "That is why I'm going to sleep on the couch tonight. You take the bed. We are technically on a first date still."

I search his dark eyes to see if he's joking. Most men I know think they are funnier than they are—they aren't. When he holds my gaze in silence, I speak. "You can't be serious." I stomp around him toward the window, not wanting to stare into his stupidly handsome face, no longer wanting to see what is being denied. "This is silly. We've already..." I can't say the words.

"Which is why I think we should wait. It'll make the next time that more special."

"What the actual. It's funny you think there is going to be a next time." I mutter the unconvincing line, not even believing it myself.

"If we're going to go the distance, Angie, one night shouldn't matter," he counters.

"My history says otherwise." I feel the weight of the chip on my shoulder, and I realize I sound like a two-year-old. The last thing a man like Brayton needs is to be worried about taking care of me. Both my hands rise to my head, and I scratch my scalp. I stare out at the lights from the sleepy town that doesn't care what struggles two people in a hotel room face.

I take a long cleansing breath and spin to face him. "You certainly are a man full of surprises."

"It doesn't sound like that's a good thing." He steps to me, his index finger landing underneath my chin. He tips it up, forcing me to look at him. "Do you understand what I'm attempting to do here? You have no idea how difficult this is," he says as his gaze lowers and locks in on my cleavage. "Especially with you dressed like this. Can I get you one of my T-shirts to sleep in?"

"Not a chance in hell," I return. I undo the one button holding the shirt together and let it slip off my shoulders down to floor. The cool hotel air runs up my bare legs, and I'm thankful I didn't remove my panties. "I think I'll prance around like this until you fall asleep."

His lips pucker into a whistle, but no sound escapes. "Something tells me I'm not going to get any sleep tonight."

"I thought that was the plan to begin with." I cross my arms against my chest just underneath my boobs, pushing them up and together. Brayton takes a stumbling step back and attempts to divert his gaze. Each time he does, it somehow ends up right back on my bosom. "Do you like what you see?"

His eyes scan me up and down and up again, never settling for longer than a second or two. "You're not going to make this easy for me, are you?"

I shake my head and turn to face the window, allowing him to take a full-on gander of my backside. "Nope. I'm going to do the complete opposite and make it extremely... hard."

I turn slowly when I hear the crash. Brayton lies on the floor, elbows propping him up, his eyes still in my direction, a foot on the top of the coffee table he must've stepped backward without looking and had tripped over.

"You've made your point, Brayton. I get it. We're two adults—I'm not nineteen years old. We can both sleep with one another and work on a relationship at the same time. Why are you fighting something we both obviously desire? Something we both want. Something we both know we'll enjoy."

He remains stretched out on the floor. He pulls his legs close to his chest and wraps his arms around across his knees, staring at the floor in front of his feet. "I'm doing a shit job of explaining my reasons, but this is something I feel is necessary. Angie, I like you. More than I think I even realize. I'd like for us to walk a little together. Can you do that for me?"

His words finally reach me. I understand what he's attempting to do. The twenty-five-year-old version of me would appreciate this gesture. I should be applauding his actions. He's showing me he's not the typical guy. He's not here just for the hookup. He's trying to have his actions match his words.

"Fine." I scoop up his shirt, hooking it over my arm. "I'm going to leave the bedroom door open. If you change your mind, there'll be a warm spot on the bed next to me for you." My gaze locks with his, and he gives me a slow nod. I hope he understands the mere suggestion of the sleeping arrangements is good enough for me. I get it, I see him, I appreciate the thought. It's the type of action a woman finds attractive. And that's the issue.

He's showing me he's a true gentleman. That is all well and good, but at the end of a beautiful date, a woman also has wants and needs.

"And, oh," I add, stepping to the doorway. I bend over knowing he's tracking my every movement. I slowly remove my panties. "I sleep in the nude. Have a good evening."

I toss the undergarment at him and turn, not needing to see his reaction. The sound of his body hitting the floor is the world's best lullaby that will be rocking me to sleep.

Chapter Ten

M y phone buzzes, and I reach across to the nonexistent nightstand. When my hand falls to the side of the bed, I open my eyes to the still-empty bed and recall the strange ending to my evening. The bedroom door is now closed, and I wonder if it's because Brayton needed to put a barrier between us. You know, me being too irresistible and all—at least, that's what my bruised ego tells me.

My phone rattles across the top of the dresser, forcing me out of the bed. I reach the phone and jump back when I notice movement on the far side of the floor. A pair of bare dark brown feet stick out from underneath a beige throw blanket.

I step around the bed and take in Brayton laid across the floor, one pillow under his head, facedown on the floor. The alarm has him stirring.

"Funny meeting you here," I tease and sit on the edge of the bed, poking his exposed leg with the tips of my toes.

"Morning, sunshine." He rolls over and runs a hand through his hair, staring up at me. When that sexy smirk appears, I realize what he is staring at—me in my birthday suit, nude.

I start to reach for the blanket and realize it's nothing he's not seen already. "If you really wanted to get a close-up look, you should've climbed into the bed last evening."

He rises from the floor, his blanket dropping away. He sleeps topless, the ripples of his six-pack causing my body to react. Thank god he's wearing tight black boxers, or I would no longer be responsible for my reaction.

"Don't you think I thought about it a few dozen times? Made it as far as the floor before reminding myself I'm a gentleman."

My eyes roam his profile as he bends over to retrieve the pillow and blanket. There should be a law for a man this kind to look this good. "You are definitely all man, but gentle isn't what I had in mind," I tease and stand, hands on my hips, hoping to get from him this morning something he denied me last evening.

I place a finger on the center of his chest, my nail scratching downward. His body reacts to my touch. "Now that we've proven we can make it through a night without attacking each other, let's move on to the next part of our relationship: lovemaking at sunrise."

The corner of his lips pulls up into a bright smile, and I know we are finally on the same page. He wraps me into a hug and kisses the top of my forehead. "How much time do you have before your shift starts?"

I place a palm on his chest. "Not enough time to do everything I want with you, but..." I push him, and he falls back onto the bed, bouncing with a lecherous grin plastered on his face. "More than enough to hold us over until we can do this again tonight."

I climb onto the bed and straddle him. He bends up and kisses me on the lips. "Mmmm, so my plan worked. You've just asked to see me again."

I lower myself onto him, returning the kiss with an intensity that speaks to my need. "Again and again and again," I repeat, hoping he hears my want.

We have limited time both today and in this relationship. As much as I like Brayton and am enjoying our time together, we both continue to ignore the fact that he lives in another state and travels constantly. We'll deal with that reality soon enough. For now, I'm more than happy enough to live in a fantasy where I get to have this incredible man in my arms, in my bed, night after night and all the mornings too.

***

I'm only five minutes late for my rounds, but it's five minutes later than I've been in my professional career. Nurse Chin shadows me through my first four patients, a look of curiosity on her face.

"Got it. We'll make sure the discharge papers are ready for Miss Moore by the time her husband arrives," she repeats back to me as I exit the patient's room. "Is there anything else you need to let me know?" she asks, and I know immediately it has nothing to do with the patients.

My professional face is plastered tight on my face, and I shake my head to the side. "Nothing else. I think we are all set. I'll be assisting in the OR with Dr. Langdon at eleven. Please confirm the bed for the patient after they complete their post-op recovery."

She nods and bites her tongue.

"What is it? What aren't you saying?" I finally ask her.

"Dr. Morgan stopped by earlier," she says bashfully.

I spin toward her. "And you are just now telling me."

"He called up early, and I told him you always arrive at least twenty minutes before rounds, so he just came up. Something to do with your consult, I believe."

"What about it?"

Her shoulders rise. "I don't know. He hung around until the start of your shift, and when you weren't here, he headed back downstairs. He said for me not to say anything to you. That he'll reach out later. Has he?"

I scan the iPad for any internal communications from the hospital intranet and come up empty. I then whip out my phone, and it's empty of any message from him there as well. "I'm sure he got pulled into something in the ER. I'll head down once I finish rounds," I say, hoping to deflect the concern I feel in my bones. I left Reggie knee-deep in medical research last evening to go on a date with Brayton. If he showed up early wanting to discuss Floyd first thing, he must've discovered something. I pray for Brayton and Floyd's sake it's something good.

I step to the next patient's room and notice Nurse Chin backing away. "Is that why you were shadowing me this morning? Because of Dr. Morgan?"

She nods, and I don't dare say anything further. The head nurses on each floor are a tight clique. They talk and gossip like no one's business. "Thank you for letting me know. I won't say a word to Dr. Morgan." I try to ease her concern and turn toward the room. I take a deep breath when Nurse Chin doesn't follow me.

There are only three additional patients on my rounds this morning, and I can't wait to rush through and get to the ER. Concern fills me. The head ER physician doesn't hang around the Ortho Unit for twenty minutes unless he has pressing news. The fact that he didn't put it in a text or email but wanted to discuss it in person sets off warning bells.

These are the actions of a doctor with bad news.

***

It takes me nearly an hour to complete my rounds. I inform Nurse Chin that I'm headed to the ER, and she merely nods. I'm sure she's already chatted with Nurse Reynolds in the ER and probably has more information about Dr. Morgan than I currently do. I ignore the gossip mill and head to the elevator.

When I step out and enter the ER, it is relatively quiet. It usually is at this early hour. Nurse Reynolds spots me and quirks her neck toward the doctors' lounge. Yes, the gossip mill runs strong at Eastport General.

I push through the door, and Reggie has his back pressed against the wall, a cup of coffee in his hand, surrounded by two nurses. They hang on his every word, stars in their eyes, tipping on their toes, leaning toward him. His fan club has recruited two new members. It boggles my mind that he continues to hit on me when he fills his cup hourly on this floor.

The ladies break into a loud laugh as if Reggie is Kevin Hart performing at the LA Coliseum. He's not. He glances over the shoulder of one of the nurses, finally spotting me. He tips his coffee at the nurses and excuses himself. The humor in his eyes fades as he approaches.

"I guess you heard I was looking for you," he starts with his greeting. "I thought you had a rule about arriving early for rounds. I guess I heard wrong."

I bite down on my lower lip to keep from exploding and remember where I'm at. The ER is Dr. Morgan's domain. He has seniority over me, and I've been brought in just for a consult. "Apologies for missing you earlier. I was..." I begin to spin a lie, but he interrupts with a wave of his hand.

"Let's go to my office. I have an update on our patient." He steps through the nurses' station and provides an update to Nurse Reynolds. When we reach the office, he holds the door open. "I get it. You have a life outside the hospital." He spits the words with an intent to spread guilt. It's a slight I hadn't expected from him.

As a female physician, I've had to overcompensate to show my focus. So many male doctors dismiss up-and-coming female physicians, joking behind our backs and sometimes to our faces that we're just here until we start popping out kids or find a husband. We can't explode back at these Neanderthals, not without having the label of emotionally unstable being added to our file.

I'm shocked Dr. Morgan harbors these thoughts. My dad has reamed out more than a few male doctors whenever he sniffed a whiff of this type of attitude. I'm surprised he didn't set Reggie straight during his residency, just another example of my dad not being infallible.

Reggie brushes past me and plops hard onto his office chair.

"You have an update?" I pivot us away from the chill in the air.

His teeth grind for a split second before he speaks. "After you left last evening, I continued to research, and I discovered Floyd is one of the top high school athletes in the country."

I nod. "Yeah, before the injury, he was projected to go top twenty in the baseball draft." I speak without thinking.

Reggie's brow pinches, the corners of his eyes tightening. "Since when are you such a baseball fan?"

I attempt to backtrack. "We knew he was here in Rhode Island for a baseball tournament."

"Yes, we did, like dozens pass through every year. I thought we just had another delusional parent who thought they were raising the next Lebron. I didn't put much stock into Brayton's claims—hell, my mom told everyone when I was sixteen I was going to find the cure for cancer. However, I looked him up and Floyd's the real deal. He's not some high schooler playing in a baseball tournament because they are bored or need the extracurricular activity for their college application and a world-class athlete. That set off a whole different set of warning bells in my head."

My arms cross, and I lean back into the chair, my breathing going shallow. Reggie didn't come looking for me with news. My mind whips to thoughts of Brayton and how much he and Floyd need a win right now. "Okay, what is the current hypothesis?"

"In retrospect, it's obvious. If Floyd was a professional ballplayer and he came in with these symptoms, it would be one of the first things we would have suspected." Reggie's gaze intensifies, as if he's challenging me to see what should be evident. He's laid enough bread crumbs for me to see where he is headed, but I refuse to believe it.

"Steroids? You must be kidding. He's only seventeen," I spit back.

"We've seen it in athletes younger. Tennis players, gymnasts." Reggie rattles off the two most prominent sports where we've seen this type of abuse in young kids. "Loser parents trying to relive their glory days through their kids, looking to give them every advantage to succeed. No matter the cost." Reggie's statement is a blanket indictment.

"Brayton would never do that," I defend the man whose bed I climbed out of a few hours ago.

Reggie scoffs. "Why is that, Angie? How could you possibly know that about a stranger? Unless..."

My head shake is too small to hide my eye roll. "What is it about you and Brayton? Are you that insecure? I saw your fan club in the break room—aren't you getting enough attention already?"

"You don't get it, do you?" he shoots back. "This changes everything, Angie. This isn't a simple kid with an injury. This is one of the country's top amateur athletes. This case is going to get flagged by the administration, just as they do for any potential high-profile patients. As his doctors, we have an obligation to file a medical report to the baseball league prior to the draft. It's nonnegotiable. And if we find steroids, we must report that too. There is no way around it. His career will be over before it starts."

My eyes close, and I try to process the news. Brayton would never give such a destructive drug to his son just to get a leg up on performance. The panic of Floyd's voice echoes in my head. The fear of losing the house, the financial peril that has hung over their family's head for years. Would that be enough pressure to make them take such a risk? Reggie's words chip away at my confidence.

Reggie's loud exhale forces me to open my eyes. "Needless to say, with the increased scrutiny we can expect from the administration, it may be wise for you to back off whatever it is going with the legal guardian and person making medical decisions for Floyd while he is still under our care." Reggie's gaze softens for the first time since we entered the room, and I begin to understand his attitude from earlier. He's not only upset I've started something with Brayton that he'd been desiring but is also trying to protect me.

"There is..."

Once again, he raises a hand, stopping me from spewing a lie we both know was coming. "Save it, Angie. Let's treat our patient. I had him moved from the ER. He's in room 812. Do you have time to join me as I try to get their consent to test for steroids? I am fully capable of getting it on my own, but I think you seeing their reaction when I ask may be the best medicine I can prescribe to help you get over whatever this is you have with Brayton."

I bite my tongue. Reggie is an experienced doctor who has seen thousands of cases. I've known Brayton for only a couple of days but can't believe he would be capable of such an abuse. I don't know what to trust, Reggie's instincts or Brayton's character.

"Let's go," I mutter. Time to find out.

***

We enter Floyd's new room, and Reggie sets an all-business mood with a mumbled "Good morning," grabbing the chart from the end of the bed and ignoring their gazes.

I tiptoe in and make eye contact with Brayton, who is sitting in the guest chair. He's chewing on a sandwich—peanut butter and jelly—a homemade sandwich which Brayton quickly tosses on top of the Ziploc bag on the chair and covers it with a magazine. He rises with a smile on his face, and I shoot him a short head shake. I cross my arms in front of me and stare at the foot of the bed, but not before seeing a confused look sweep across his face.

Floyd's new room is a standard hospital room. It's a double, but the second bed is vacant. Mylar balloons sit on the windowsill along with a matching set of hospital flowers Brayton handed me last evening. In my haste to get home and change and get to the hospital, I realize I left the flowers in his hotel room. I wonder if this is the same set.

"How's our patient this morning?" Reggie asks. It's a formality as he continues to scan the chart, not expecting a response.

Floyd shifts up in the bed, his eyes wide as his gaze flashes from Reggie to his dad before returning to Reggie. "Okay, I guess," Floyd whispers, fear in his voice.

"Is everything okay?" Brayton says, stepping to the side of his son's bed, his hands squeezing the metal bar. He's wearing a T-shirt advertising a construction company and those damn sexy jeans from the bar on our first night.

It takes everything in me not to wrap my arms around him. "Vitals are strong, and the pain meds appear to be working," I say, buying Reggie time to complete his review of the overnight chart.

Reggie stuffs the chart under his arm. "Mr. Patterson," he addresses Brayton, "as I mentioned to you last evening, we have ruled out a number of possible causes for your son's condition, including cancer."

"Yes, that's good, right?" Brayton takes his son's hand into his and squeezes tight.

"It's progress," Reggie returns. "We're still investigating, and until we discover the cause of the loss of bone density, we fear Floyd may continue to risk fractures or worse, a full break."

A flash of shock races across Brayton's face before he realizes Floyd is looking at him. He quickly steels his expression and denies his feelings from showing. Just another sacrifice he makes in the name of being a parent. "I can..." He struggles for the right words. "We'll eliminate anything physical, no practices. Does he need to stay home from school? How long will it take to discover...?"

Reggie raises a palm. "Let's not get too far ahead of ourselves. There are additional tests we'd like to run which may be able to clarify things. It does require, however, consent."

Brayton's face freezes, and I step in. "Brayton, we ask only because it affects how we treat Floyd. We are all on the same page. We want to make Floyd better."

"What are you asking, Angie?" He calls me by my first name, the familiar name, and I twist away from Reggie, not wanting to read his reaction.

I take a step toward the bed, my hand squeezing Floyd's ankle. "Floyd, is there any possibility you've taken steroids?"

Confusion fills his face, and he turns to his father.

"Are you shitting me?" Brayton explodes, releasing his son's hand. I take a step back and bump into an approaching Reggie.

I raise my hands in front of me. "I'm not saying willingly."

"Although we aren't ruling that out either," Reggie says behind me.

I shoot a *not helping* glare over my shoulder at him before turning to face a still-fuming Brayton. "Could he have mistakenly taken something that may contain a steroid? It could be a supplement, a special vitamin from a teammate. Anything? It would help us with our investigation."

Reggie steps in front of me. "Just to be clear. Given the impact to the bones, this would not have been a onetime accidental dosing. We are looking at prolonged exposure," Reggie piles on, practically calling them cheats. "Floyd? Is there anything you aren't telling us?"

Brayton squeezes his son's hand. "Son, you don't have to answer that question." He takes a protective papa bear stance. "I can't believe you guys would even ask that." Eyes ablaze, he points over Reggie's shoulder at me. "Especially you, Angie."

He shakes his head. "I'd never do anything that would jeopardize my son. Floyd would never take a shortcut in life. That's not who we are. We work hard and keep our heads down."

"We didn't mean to—" I start.

"But you did," he snaps back. "Everything Floyd has achieved on the baseball field has been through his talent, skill, and hard work. We play by the rules on the field and off."

I hear him, and I understand. "We didn't mean to imply..." I begin to defend our position. From a clinical perspective, it's a necessary data point. Not every patient plays by the rules. Many of them abuse themselves to the point of addiction, some so out of control they are too far gone by the time they arrive at the hospital.

"We hear you, Brayton," Reggie attempts to pull us back, "but look at it from our position. Your son has a condition consistent with steroid abuse. He's a world-class athlete and wouldn't be the first baseball player to swear to the heavens they are clean while popping pills before every game." I cringe at his phrasing, wondering if he's looking for Brayton to take a swing at him.

"With all due respect," Brayton says, straightening his back and taking a step toward Reggie, the veins in his neck visible, "my son isn't just any ballplayer. He is my life. I would have to be the most cynical asshole on the planet to make all the sacrifices we've made as a family to get us this far, to begin to cheat this close. Are you calling me an asshole, Doc?"

Floyd's eyes go wide as he fists the sheets on the bed. He knows his father better than anyone in this room, and I fear for Reggie's life.

"Let's all take a beat," I say, stepping around Reggie and in front of Brayton. His shoulders slump, and his body relaxes. He steps back to the bed, hands resting on the metal bar.

"Is this what both of you think of us? The poor family from Springfield that must cheat to get ahead?" Anger has left his body, replaced with something that is even worse. A heart-breaking sadness.

Floyd reaches up to his dad's hand and squeezes it. The steroid accusation may be new to them, but I get the sense they have been fighting battles like this all their lives. Fighting together.

"We'll come back once you've had a chance to calm down." I begin to turn when I feel a slight pull on my elbow.

"I thought you believed in me. I thought you understood, Angie." Brayton's words halt my exit, my body stiffening in place. My name on his lips causes me to lower my guard.

"It's not about what I believe, Brayton," I speak as my voice cracks. "It's what the science shows." I step back toward the bed. "Believing in people is an admirable trait, but it comes with heartache and disappointment." A vision of my dad flashes before my eyes. "You can know someone literally your entire life and never suspect they would do something that would go against their principles, would go against everything they've ever taught you. But it happens."

I feel the heat in my chest, in my cheeks, the emotions of that moment years ago pushing its way back up. I take an audible breath and attempt to clear my mind. Reggie's words from earlier ring in my ears. This case is going to be carefully watched by the administration. I know what is expected. I know what the rules state. I have no choice.

"In my profession, we speak of trust, but we make damn sure to verify. So I'm sorry if two experienced, competent doctors attempting to get to the root cause of a medical mystery have to ask you a couple of tough questions. I'm sorry if it ruffles your delicate sensibilities. I'm sorry we unfortunately don't live in the land of taking a person at his word or believing in rainbows and fairy dust. We are all adults here living in a real world."

Reggie steps behind me, his hands landing on my shoulders. It's a move meant to support me, but it's an unnecessary move. I'm a damn good physician and don't need his approval to know I've handled this delicate situation.

His warm breath floats over my shoulder toward Brayton. "We'll give you a few moments to lick your wounds, and when we return, we'll be more than happy to have an adult conversation with you."

Brayton grinds his teeth so hard I fear he's going to break a molar. But I don't react, and I don't wait for a response from him. I turn to walk away but not before he grunts.

"Give me the damn papers and I'll sign. And once these waste-of-time tests come back clean, we'll be looking to get discharged. I believe we no longer have a reason to stay in Eastport."

I freeze, his words hitting me hard.

"Great. We'll send in the nurse with the paperwork." Reggie's words snap me out of my trance, his tap on the top of my shoulders indicating for me to follow.

I take a final gaze at Brayton, who turns away from me to whisper to his son. I stop at the doorway and chance another glance, hoping he looks my way. He doesn't.

I push through the door, chest heaving, pulse racing. I stop next to the nurses' station as Reggie sidles up next to me. He begins a soft, slow clap that grows in intensity, volume, and cadence.

A few of the nurses notice, and I lower my chin to chest and attempt to hide behind my hair. I wave a hand in his direction and direct him toward the lounge. I wait for the door to close before turning to face him.

I feel like crap, and Reggie has a pompous shit-eating grin plastered on his face. "That, Dr. Carmichael, was freaking awesome. I didn't know you had it in you."

I look over his shoulder toward the closed door. "That was totally unprofessional. I should..."

"You should bask in the glory of your greatness. Did you catch the look on his face when you delivered that smackdown?" Reggie reveals another part of himself. An unattractive, nonsympathetic part.

"I shouldn't have pushed him so hard. If the tests come back clean and he leaves, we'll be no closer to helping them. Why didn't you stop me?"

Reggie leans against the same wall he had the last time I entered the lounge. It must be his favorite spot. "It was nice not having to play the bad cop for once." A sneer spreads across his face. "If he didn't agree, I would have found a way to draw a sample and test."

"You can't be serious right now. How can you say that? To me of all people." I can't believe my ears.

His brow pinches in confusion. It's obvious he hasn't been paying attention if he's shocked this is my response.

"We can't order a new test without the patient's consent. You know this. There are rules in place for a reason."

He pushes out a dismissive scoff. "Yeah, the reason is to save the hospital from lawsuits. I'm more interested in saving lives."

"And how many lives can you save if you have your medical license suspended or, even worse, revoked? How many lives may be impacted if the hospital has to pay off a lawsuit and then delays upgrading medical equipment in the ER? How many lives has my dad been able to save since he lost his license?" I say the words I wish I had the opportunity to tell Dad before he acted so recklessly. Before he turned his life upside down. "Think before you act. You can't just do what you want in the moment because that's what your ego demands."

"Oh really?" Reggie pushes off the wall and strides toward me. "Sometimes you can overthink a situation when the clues are laid out right in front of you, the answer as clear as a blue summer sky. It must be so hard going around life with a foot hovering over the brake, hands clenched tight to the steering wheel, afraid of letting go and feeling the rush of doing something your heart knows it wants to do. Something you know will feel so right."

He says the line like an entitled man used to getting his way. I wish he could live in high heels for twenty-four hours and see the roadblocks thrown in front of a woman on a daily basis. He'd realize being so blasé about infractions is not an option, one mistake and you are seen as a liability.

He bites down on his lower lip. The movement forces my eyes to follow. Reggie knows he's an attractive man but fails to see not every woman is bowled over by an alpha attitude and persistence.

I'm the first to blink. I take a tiny step back in order to breathe. "We are having a passionate conversation about our patient, and you use it to twist it to yet another 'Reggie wants to get into Angie's pants' session?"

"You're not wearing pants," he growls, my words rolling off him like melting ice on a Colorado mountain in the spring.

"And you are totally missing my point."

He reaches forward, the tips of his finger landing on the collar of my blouse. "When it comes to you, Angie, I don't miss much. I heard the passion in your voice. You may be afraid to break a rule to get what you want, but something tells me you want me to prove to you that it's okay to go after what you want. So..." His finger runs along up my collar until it reaches my earlobe. He flicks it gently before his hand cups me by the back of my head.

"You do know what they call a man who acts without consent," I whisper.

His smirk confirms to me that he's clueless as to what is about to happen. "I think the proper term is take charge. Or is it lucky?"

I pull back from him, wanting to get a clear view of his reaction when I speak. "Nope. The proper term is fired."

He freezes in place. His brow pinches as he attempts to read me. To see if I'm joking.

"Let go of me, Reggie, and let's get back to work." His hand lowers, and I almost feel bad when a look of shame, confusion, and regret sweep across his face. Like I said—almost.

His silence is my best reward. I step around him and peer over my shoulder as I hold open the door. "I'll be upstairs in Ortho. Ping me when we have the test results back."

I start to march to the elevator and pause by the nurses' station. It barely registers when Reggie walks by into the elevator, headed back to the ER.

A wave of regret sweeps over me. Like it did with Brayton, my history of not being taken seriously forced me to do something potentially destructive. I overcompensated, nearly threatened to have the head of the ER fired. I'm sure the fallout will be massive.

In the span of twenty minutes, I've destroyed my relationship with not one but two men. I turn back toward Floyd's hospital room. Maybe I'm not too late to salvage one of them.

Chapter Eleven

I knock and enter Floyd's hospital room and find the guest chair empty.

"He went for a walk," Floyd's gravelly voice greets me. His eyelids flutter, but he maintains eye contact.

My lips part, and I click my tongue against the top teeth. "I'll come back later."

"Not believing my dad is probably the worst thing you could ever do to him," Floyd continues, and I step further into the room. The door squeaks closed behind me. His gaze dives to his lap, but he forces out the words. "All my life he's told me if you don't have your word, you don't have anything."

I tamp down the need to react. I'm not here to debate with a seventeen-year-old. I'll listen, hoping to get an insight Brayton hasn't shared.

Floyd pushes up from the bed, yet his gaze continues to avoid me. "When I was twelve years old, my dad drove ten counties over from our home because a white baseball coach happened to see me play in a Little League game. The coach had told my dad I had more talent and potential than any kid he'd come across in the entire state in the last five years. He convinced my dad he'd give me a spot on his squad, which happened to be the two-time defending champions in the area. All we had to do was find a way for me to get to the games." Floyd's eyes glaze over in remembrance as he adjusts the pillow behind his lower back, settling into the story.

"In our small hometown, I was already playing with boys three and four years older than me. My dad saw this as an opportunity for me to grow, push myself, and be taught by coaches that had played baseball in college and, in some cases, the minor leagues. Better instruction than was available in our neighborhood." Floyd stops himself from calling his neighborhood poor, but I already know life has presented challenges for the both of them.

"Dad juggled his schedule, like he always does, and drove me. When we arrived at the field, the coach greeted us and introduced us to the rest of the team. It was, to no one's surprise, one hundred percent white. Kids with trust funds, gloves worth more than my entire outfit, and thirty or forty parents in the stands even for practice. All things that would make a kid like me nervous. But I wasn't. My dad had taught me from the time I could walk that no person was any better or worse than me because of how they looked, where they grew up, or how much money they had." A look of pride fills his face, just the latest example of the wonderful job Brayton has done with his son.

"I raced out to the field and was met by one of the assistant coaches. He took one look at me with my six-year-old worn-out glove and thrift market sweatpants and told me I had to try out for the squad.

"I shrugged my shoulders and proceeded to walk to the pitcher's mound. I was only twelve, but all my life I had been asked to prove I belonged. It kind of goes with the territory when you are a black person in America."

My shoulders sag in understanding. An all-too-familiar scene that is repeated across this great country every single day. Even a twelve-year-old boy is unable to avoid it. It's an onerous journey for any person, which I can relate to. Being a black woman, whose father was already a doctor, I think of all the whispers and snickers behind my back growing up and throughout medical school, people questioning my right to be where I was.

"To this day, I remember the sound of my father's voice." Floyd's voice drops to a baritone, a poor imitation of his father. "Boy, go get in the car. We are going home." He pauses, his chin rising and his gaze finally capturing mine. "The coach raced to my dad and asked him what he was doing, especially after driving that far. My dad looked him in the eye and said, 'You said he had a spot on the club. All he needed to do was find a way here. He's here. He's not a show horse—you've already seen him play. Are you a man who stands by his words or not? If not, then it's best to know right now because I won't have my son around a coach whose word means nothing.'"

A smile spreads across Floyd's face, and I can picture Brayton standing tall, standing proud, spouting those words. "I wasn't nervous, I wasn't scared. I had never been prouder of my dad."

Floyd pauses his story at the sound of the squeak of the door behind me.

"That team was the Plymouth Hens, and they went on to win two more championships with Floyd leading the way. No team in the state's history had ever done that before or since." Brayton's soft voice floats in the air. He steps in and nods at his son. He turns to face me. "I'm sorry for nearly taking off your head, Angie."

"And I'm sorry for insinuating you'd ever do anything harmful to you, son. This test will help us, all of us."

He nods. "I needed that walk to calm down. I ended up in the lobby. I saw all the plaques of the doctors down there. All the awards the hospital has won. I apologize. I get a little worked up when it comes to Floyd. I should have taken you at your word."

"And we should have read the situation a little better and walked you through our rationale. We wouldn't be doing our jobs if we didn't explore everything. There are so many chemicals and additives in society today, he could've ingested something without his knowledge. You must know we are just trying to get to the root cause so we can focus on getting Floyd better." Our eyes lock, and I sense Brayton reading into my soul, determining what type of person I am. Will my actions be in concert with my words? He blinks, a nearly unperceivable nod of his head, telling me he believes me. I exhale. "I'm glad we can get past this and move forward," I offer.

Brayton steps to me and lowers his voice, his words only meant for me. "I feel so bad. How can I make it up to you?"

I shake my head. "We're good, Brayton. They'll run the tests overnight, and we should have the results first thing in the morning."

Brayton extends the tips of both his fingers toward me. I glance over his shoulder at Floyd, who appears focused on his phone. I pull on the wide lapels of my lab coat, hoping he understands. I'm at work. Reassuring a family member or patient may be part of the job, but the type of comforting Brayton is seeking is outside of any professional conduct.

He lowers his hands, and his gaze intensifies. "Let me make it up to you for dinner tonight. Visiting hours end at..."

I shake my head. "I don't think is a good idea, Brayton. We've already..."

"Don't say it."

My feet step back, and my back presses against the door. Brayton's steps mirror mine. "I think we should take a break, Brayton, and focus on Floyd."

His eyes flash for a second before he leans forward, his forehead a mere inch from mine. "Don't do that. Floyd is in this hospital room all night. I can't stay with him. My evening is free. I assume so is yours. Why can't we get back to getting to know each other?"

"It's not that simple. I'm your son's doctor. It's not..." I fumble for the right words. Usually, I can hide behind a rule, but that isn't the case here. "It's just... complicated."

"You're a black physician living in Rhode Island. Something tells me complications have never been a challenge for you before." His words strike a nerve. In my professional career, I never shy away from a challenge, so why do I do it in my personal life? I always choose to retreat rather than fight. Easier to troll a local bar once a month than fight for a relationship. "Give me your word, Angie. Just tell me you aren't interested in me, and I'll stop. I'll believe whatever it is you say. I trust you."

I can't look away from his needy eyes, the sense of want rolling off him, making me feel weak. I take a cleansing breath and prepare to speak my truth...

Chapter Twelve

I t's like déjà vu all over again, yet so different. I exit the elevator, this time dressed in the casual outfit I wore today: a comfortable pair of black cotton-blend slacks, a teal blouse, and flats. It's seven fifty-nine in the evening, and I want to enjoy a quiet moment in the Eastport General Hospital lobby before Brayton arrives.

When Brayton looked at me earlier, I realized that if I walked away I'd regret it. He has more belief in an us than I do, but isn't that what it's going to take for someone with my history? I have to see this through.

Without thinking my feet take me to the wall of plaques, the gold-embossed tributes to the hospital greats of the past. Some of the names I've met, most I've only heard stories about. It's been a year, yet the spot I've stared at every day since I've started at Eastport remains blank. The spot that once held my father's plaque.

"Impressive wall." His deep baritone voice snaps me out of the rabbit hole I always fall into when thinking about the mess my dad created.

I twist to face him, and his eyes lower to what I hold in my hand. "I didn't hear you walk up."

His eyes flicker up to meet mine, a slight smirk on his face. "You appeared lost in thought." He points to the gift shop flowers I'm holding. "Are those for me?"

I extend them toward him. "Last night you planned the date. Tonight is my turn." Brayton is wearing the same outfit as earlier. No tight turtleneck, no blazer tonight. "Let's walk this way." I begin to stride past him, but his arm hooks around my waist.

"In a second. First this." He pulls me to his chest, his lips crashing against mine. I hadn't expected such a bold move, especially after the day we've had. My lips separate and he pushes his tongue in, a welcome addition. His tongue sweeps across mine, and I close my eyes, enjoying the moment.

What if I hadn't returned to Floyd's room—where would we be now? I forced myself to confront him when my history told me to give up and go the other way. And now he's here in my arms. And he feels damn good.

I scan my mind—if anyone else attempted such a bold move, in the lobby of my place of work no less, I would feel self-conscious—and look to walk away. But with Brayton, I embrace it. He's making me forget my history. I ignore the echoes of footsteps around us; I ignore what I know are the stares of the security guards on duty. With Brayton, everything I thought I knew feels different.

"Now that's the proper way to start a date." Brayton has no filter when it comes to me. From the moment we've met, he's been relentless. I wait for signs that it's a game for him, I wait for his excitement of the chase to shift to boredom, I wait for him to show that he's just like every other guy I've met, and I am constantly surprised. He's still here. He still wants me.

He hooks his arm, and I slip my hand through and lead him to the elevator. "We're not leaving the building?"

I shake my head. "Last night you shared your world. Tonight, I get to show you mine. Just so you don't get your hopes up, it's not nearly as exciting as country line dancing."

His chuckle bounces off the wall of the elevator. "If it's your world, I'm sure it's just as amazing." His hand slips into mine, and I don't resist it, even after the elevator doors open. "Hey, I recognize this floor. Don't tell me your idea of a dinner date is..."

I giggle like the schoolgirl he makes me feel like. "Yup, the cafeteria."

"Wow, when you said not to raise my expectations, you weren't kidding. I've eaten lunch here, and news flash, it tastes just like hospital food."

We push through the doors to a quiet cafeteria. With visiting hours ending, this side of the cafeteria closes in less than an hour. But it's not this side I want to show him. I step through the employee entrance, behind the counter, and continue into the kitchen. "Most meals in a hospital are prepared with little additives, minimal salt, pepper, butter, sugar for a reason. Most of the patients are on restricted diets, and we know family members will bring them food from the cafeteria, hence the flavor."

"I've never thought of that." Brayton nods, taking in the massive kitchen.

"The kitchen staff is actually very well-trained; the chefs have all graduated culinary school." I navigate him around the two-thousand-square-foot kitchen. "Meals are prepared eighteen hours a day, seven days a week. It's a grueling schedule with no days off." Brayton's eyes brighten as he takes in the information few people ever consider.

We step around two members of the janitorial services team, and I knock on the frame of the open office door with the name Chef Marian Bethel. "Dr. Carmichael." Marian looks up from her desk, pen in hand and a pile of paper underneath her. "I was surprised by your request this evening." Chef Marian stands. She is white, dark-haired with a streak of gray, mid-forties, with a warm smile on her face. She glances over my shoulder, taking in Brayton, her brows rising. "Now I understand."

"Chef Marian, this is my... friend Brayton Patterson." I step to the side, and the pair exchanges handshakes. I turn to face Brayton. "When I first started here at Eastport, I would come down to the cafeteria every night after shift with a pile of files and grab dinner and work," I begin to explain.

"All the young doctors start out this way. Working way too many hours, never getting proper rest, never eating a proper meal," Marian embellishes. "Her dad—what a wonderful man—asked me to keep an eye on her. When I came to find out she spent more time in the hospital than anyone who wasn't a patient, we made an agreement."

Marian hooks a supportive arm around my shoulder. "She made me promise that if I'm working late to call down and she'll prepare a proper, flavorful, healthy meal for me."

"She lives on nuts and energy bars all day. Dinner is the only proper meal she ever eats," Marian outs me. My day is too hectic, and I always forget to eat, my schedule only allowing me to nibble.

"And coffee. Plenty of coffee," I add.

"It's good to see you. We missed you last evening," she says. Her gaze, however, is directed at Brayton as if she's already deciphered the mystery. "Come this way. Your meals await." We follow her through the kitchen to a raised counter with heat lamps attached. Most of the lamps are off at this hour except for two near the end. "I've prepared your favorites."

My mouth begins to water as we approach, and I take in the perfectly cooked pink salmon, garlic spinach, and mashed sweet potatoes. "This is perfect. How can I ever thank you?"

"Just have your father pop by. It's been too long."

I merely nod and plaster a fake smile on my face. Everywhere I go in the hospital, I am reminded that I am my father's child. Marian would be surprised how long it's been since I've last seen my father, our last conversation evolving into a nonproductive shout fest.

Marian laughs and extends her hand toward Brayton, shaking it once again. "Take care of this special lady. She's one of the best doctors in the hospital." She twists toward me, shooting me a wink. "You know where the trays and utensils are. Enjoy the rest of the evening, and go get some air."

Marian disappears back toward her office, and Brayton steps to me. "I see you know nice people in high places," he jokes.

"Only the best for you," I speak without thinking, the words causing both of us to pause. Brayton stares at me with deep, dark eyes, and I know I must say something before he does. "I mean, it's the least I could do given..."

His hand lands on my forearm, and a spark races up my arm. "I think you said what you meant the first time. I get the impression from the chef you don't do this for just anyone."

It takes me a beat to respond, his words revealing to me more than I want to admit. "First time. Even when I work late with other doctors, we always order takeout." The more I speak, the more I realize what I've done. "This has always been my private little secret. I've never shared it with anyone else before."

He spots the trays in the corner and grabs two, stepping back to me. "This is already better than line dancing." He places the dishes on the trays and holds them shoulder height high, with a *what comes next* smile on his face.

I mirror his look, no longer able to resist. "This way," I say, scooping up the utensils on the way toward the exit. He's made it clear he's not going anywhere. He really wants to get to know me outside the bedroom, the good and the bad.

I'll show it to him, and I'll prepare myself for when he runs away.

***

Eastport, Rhode Island, doesn't have much of a skyline. In fact, the hospital is one of the tallest buildings in the town. However, with dark skies, the twinkling stars, and soft jazz music streaming from my phone, I feel pretty good about my choice of dinner spots.

Brayton spears a forkful of greens and twirls it in front of my face. We are sitting on stolen folding chairs at a rickety plastic card table ten feet from the industrial-sized air-conditioning unit on the roof of the hospital. I've covered the table with a red paper tablecloth stolen from the children's floor. A bucket with chilled white wine sits by our feet.

"This is delicious, and I love the view. So peaceful," Brayton says with a sincerity in his voice I find surprising.

"This is where I escape to get away from the stress sometimes." I begin to explain the history of the roof. I point to a corner spot behind him. "I cried there for twenty minutes when I lost my first patient—a father of two. His kids, two girls, were only four and six years old."

I feel the tears well up as I recall that terrible day. I've lost other patients since; it always guts me, but that first one nearly had me rethinking my profession. Only my dad was able to walk me back.

Brayton lowers his fork and rests his hand on top of mine, a sympathetic look on his face. "I can't even imagine."

"Do no harm," I whisper. "That's the number one rule they teach us in medical school. It's the mantra we live by." I choke back the emotions growing inside me and push past it. "They fail to tell you that you can't save everybody. No matter how smart you think you are or how hard you work."

He takes my hand in his and pulls it up to his lips, placing a gentle kiss just below my knuckle. I point to another spot on the roof. "I was hiding there after I heard the rumors I knew couldn't be true. And then I received the phone call from my dad telling me I was wrong. It was true. He had been fired."

My eyes blink rapidly, staving off the tears for the moment, a need to see Brayton clearly overriding my need to cry. I'm about to pull back the blanket and reveal the secret that is not so secret around the hospital but one he will hear about if he's going to remain in my life.

"Your dad, he was a doctor here too, right?" Brayton asks tentatively. His instinct to proceed with caution is spot-on.

I nod. "He was the head of the ER unit."

"Like Dr. Morgan?" Brayton says, and I pull my hand from his.

"Nothing like Dr. Morgan, but yes, same position." A wave of conflicting emotions hits me. It's been a little while since I've had to talk to someone who didn't already know my dad and his history.

My shoulders hunch as my arms squeezes the sides of the chair next to my hips. "Growing up, my dad was like a superhero. A doctor who saves lives. How could you grow up in a house like that and not want to be a doctor?" I think back to Dad coming home on the good days, regaling me and Mom with tales from the hospital—how they saved a patient after a car crash, a farm accident, a construction fall. My dad played the lead role in the superhero series in my mind, his lab coat his cape, and I couldn't wait until he arrived home each night with the next exciting episode.

"I decided to become a doctor because of him. When I began my residency, he tried to get me to study under him.

I knew it was against the rules, but he went to the head administrator and somehow got it approved. I was so upset I had him reassign me to another area of the hospital.

Rules exist for a reason.

Dad was pissed, but eventually, he understood. I couldn't start my career with him moving the pieces on the chessboard for me. I had to strike out and build my career on my own." I release a long, calming breath. Those first months were exciting—I learned so much, but I also had a chance to drop in unannounced and see how Dad ran his unit. I shared drinks and the occasional lunch comparing note with the residents underneath his tutelage I discovered getting me to study under him wasn't the only rule he bent.

"A lot of doctors bend rules, they say in the name of their patient care. But it's a dangerous rabbit hole to fall into," I start. "Where does it stop? Who gives you the right to play god?" I shake my head and whisper, "Do no harm."

I tip my wineglass toward Brayton, who refills it. I take a sip and capture his gaze. He's mesmerized, and I can't believe I've already shared so much with him. "My dad says it was all hospital politics—it wasn't. He broke one of the biggest rules we have in our profession. The HIPAA privacy law."

Most people, even nonmedical people, are familiar with the United States HIPAA privacy law. You can not disclose medical details about a person without their explicit consent.

Brayton nods, and I continue, "The patient was an eighteen-month-old child. A medical mystery that confounded my dad and the other doctors. All signs pointed to a hereditary disease, but neither parent carried the markers. My dad wanted to run a DNA screening, and the mother refused. Not once, not twice, but three times." My throat catches as I recall the details of the case that took down my dad.

"The rules are clear. Two other doctors even warned my dad. But my dad didn't follow the rule book, his instinct, gut, and thirty years of experience outweighing logic and law. He stole from the garbage discarded coffee cups from the parents and ran the test without consent.

"The father wasn't the baby's biological father, something she not only kept from her husband but also my dad, who asked her in private. When my dad produced the unsanctioned DNA test, the husband confronted the mother. She admitted to multiple affairs, and he filed for divorce. She sued the hospital.

"The inquiry board, though sympathetic to my dad, fired him. He had no legal leg to stand on." I shake my head as a tear threatens to roll down my cheek.

Brayton pushes a tissue in my direction. "What became of the child?"

"With the new information, they located and tested the biological father and were able to confirm the disease. The child was treated over the next six months and made a full recovery."

"So, your dad was right." Brayton's response shocks me.

"I'm sorry, but a hundred and fifty years of medical litigation disagrees. It was a clear-cut violation. As clear-cut as it gets." I've used these same words in early discussions with my dad. How could they not see the rule violation?

"Screw the history. Your dad saved that kid's life. That was his patient, right?"

I nod.

"And don't you do everything under your control to save your patient."

"Everything legally possible. Yes," I counter. The feeling of guilt I always get when discussing my dad sweeps over me. Most daughters would defend their fathers to the end of time. But his actions had ramifications. To this day, I second-guess every one of my decisions knowing the stigma of being his daughter hangs over my head, my actions being watched and reviewed. I'm sure other doctors who worked with him, that learned under his tutelage, have all gone through a self-introspective review of how they conduct themselves. Every one of them except Reggie.

Brayton lowers his chin to his chest. "I went through something like that with my mom years ago. Not nearly as life-or-death." His voice lowers to just above a whisper, and my heart begins to thump. He's doing something most guys have issues with—he's opening up. An action that he's done since the moment I met him. "Once Floyd's mom decided she wasn't coming back, and I became a single parent, my mom, unbeknown to me, had a DNA test run on Floyd. She didn't tell me at the time."

My mouth falls open.

"It took her two months before she gave me the report." Brayton must notice the shock on my face. "I'm the father. I was furious at my mom for doing what she did at the time. Going behind my back, not believing, but as I've gotten older and have learned how protective you get with your child, I came to understand. You do what is required to protect your child." Brayton's gaze remain locked on the plate of half-eaten food in front of him. "My mom and I reconciled sometime later. She was right. If Floyd's mom could leave a beautiful child behind, what else was she capable of. Lying, cheating, who knows? My mom insisted I get full custody so that I wouldn't have to have her in my life any longer. That I wouldn't have to fear her showing up out of the blue one day, turning my world upside down. I was young and lacked her experience and perspective to understand what she was doing at the time. I only agreed when she got me to realize it would be best for Floyd. Floyd didn't need to worry the mother who abandoned him, who didn't know him, may one day show up on our doorstep and try to take him away from the only home he knew."

"She abandoned both of you," I whisper.

"Good riddance." He scoffs. "I say this to say, I understand your dad's motivation. He saved that kid's life. He cared more for that child than the mother did. That makes him a hero in my book," Brayton says with stars in his eyes. The same stars I'm sure he sees his mom in now.

I understand leading with your heart, but if everyone did that, the world would be in chaos. "You don't get it," I counter, "because of his actions that was the last life he was able to save. Because he thought he was above the law, he no longer gets to do what he loves to do. What he was put on this earth to do. Because of what he's done, every time I hear a patient expires in the ER, the second thought I have after my heart breaking for the family is whether their life could have been saved if my dad was on duty."

With my admission, the wall of tears falls. It's an admission I've never told anyone, not even my dad. It's

been over a year since my dad was walked out of the
hospital, but his shadow continues to hang heavy over the
hospital and me.

Brayton steps around the table and wraps me in his arms.
I curl into the crook of his neck, unable to stop the cascade
of tears. I know I've ruined the date, but just as important,
I've shown him how broken I truly am.

I cry because of the guilt I feel about my father, but I
cry also because I know my history. It's at this point in a
relationship, when I've opened up, when I've shown my
vulnerability and pain, that men walk away. It's why I no
longer do relationships. Yet here I am, my rule tossed to the
side for Brayton.

My tears have already ruined the date. All that's left now
is for me to brace for Brayton to tell me we are over.

Chapter Thirteen

W e exit the elevator and return the trays to the cafeteria. After my cryfest, Brayton shifted the conversation to lighter topics. His sense of caring and always knowing what I need, when I need it, on display again. He truly is a gentle soul.

Brayton distracted me with funny tales of traveling with Floyd and the behind-the-scenes drama of being a parent of a travel baseball athlete. The fart-filled hotel rooms when the kids gather; how the traveling parents have learned to stand back at the morning breakfast buffet until the kids have grabbed their food—unless they want to risk losing a limb; which parents use baseball as a way to stay on the road away from their spouse; and, of course, the highs and lows of baseball tournaments with a bunch of teens still trying to process emotions. Brayton jokes about pitching the idea as a Netflix series—the terrible teens of travel baseball.

My well-timed nods and soft smiles kept him going, but I can sense I've ruined the evening. We walk in silence back to the lobby, where I don't resist when Brayton takes my hand.

I move on autopilot and don't realize until Brayton's feet stop where he's taken me. "That's it, huh?"

We are standing in front of the wall of plaques, directly in front of the empty space. He points to the still-vacant hole where the screw holding the plaque remains. "How did you know?" I whisper, my focus on the black, white, and gray marble.

"Both nights I met you, I found you either standing in front of it or your eyes returning to this spot over and over."

How in the world did he notice something so subtle I wasn't even aware I was doing it?

"Someday, they will have a plaque here for you, Angie." His voice is filled with sincerity, and my heart swoons just a little. If only we had met under different circumstances, at a different point in my life.

"Good night, Brayton. Sorry for ruining our evening. I'll see you in the morning with Dr. Morgan." I squeeze the straps of my shoulder bag and lower my head, not wanting to see the disappointment in his eyes.

He steps forward, his hand cupping my face. His eyes stare deep into my soul. "Our evening is not done yet. You didn't ruin a goddamn thing. When you speak from your heart, you could never. You never will."

My breath escapes me, and I attempt to gather myself.

"Sharing the dark and the painful is just as important as your shiny goodness. It's how we get to truly see each other. And nothing you have shown me wants me to run and hide, Angie. In fact, it's the opposite." He presses his forehead to mine, his hands still on my face, his heated breath making my head swirl.

"This evening is far from over. I only have one question for you, and there is no wrong answer."

My eyes bat because I don't have the words to answer him.

"Your place or mine?" he whispers.

"But..." I begin to protest. Even after I've shared with him my struggles, he wants to be with me.

"'But' wasn't one of the choices," he growls.

A small voice I don't recognize escapes my mouth. "Mmm... mine." If we are truly on a journey of discovery, I might as well pull back all the curtains and flick on the lights. Only one other man has made it far enough back to my place. After him, I swore I would never bring back another.

But Brayton is unlike any man I've been with. He's got me feeling things I hadn't thought I was capable of feeling. He's got me thinking about a future that extends beyond tomorrow. I'm bringing him back to my condo after promising myself I would never do that.

Brayton Patterson is the type of man who has me breaking rules. It's early in our relationship, and I'm unsure whether this is a good thing or a bad thing.

***

My condo is within walking distance of the hospital, and I convince Brayton to leave his car in the hospital garage overnight. He wraps his muscular arms around my shoulders to protect me from the night air as we take a leisurely stroll to my building.

Brayton whistles as we approach the ten-story glass condo. I've never considered the building as more than a place to rest my head at night, but Brayton appears impressed.

Wilton, the overnight doorman, holds open the door for us. "Evening, Dr. Carmichael. Welcome back."

"Thank you, Wilton. Any packages for me?" I ask.

"Nothing today. Are you expecting anything specific? I'll keep an eye out." He races ahead to press the elevator button for us.

I shake my head. "Nothing expected," I mutter and step into the elevator. Brayton slides in next to me, and the door closes.

"I don't think I've ever been in a building with a twenty-four-hour doorman," he jokes. "What was that about a package?"

I shrug. "Given that I often work late, having a doorman building was one of the few things I required when looking for a place." I fail to answer his second question, thankful when the elevator doors open on seven.

Not even the jiggle of my keys is enough to distract him. "And the packages?"

I open the door and swing it open, holding it for him to enter. "It's silly, really."

He stops in the doorway and stares at me. "Angie? What did we say?"

"Okay, fine," I say, swinging my arms for him to enter. I close and lock the door behind him. When I turn, my gaze meets his concerned eyes, and once again, I am touched by his kindness and caring.

I lead him into my living room. It's nothing fancy. An L-shaped olive-colored couch, a large coffee table where my laptop resides with a stack of files. A curio with trinkets transitions to three large bookcases. In front of the couch is a large-screen television, which I can't recall the last time it was turned on. A wall of glass showcases the small balcony. I have two rocking chairs and a small table out there.

"Your place is beautiful," Brayton says as we pause by the glass windows, staring out at the lights. The night sky and stars always provide me a calming escape, and I get the sense it does the same for Brayton.

"The anniversary from when I graduated med school is next week," I blurt out, my voice sounding whiny. "It's silly. It was so long ago."

"Sounds like it's an important date." Brayton gives no quarter.

I turn from the window and make my way to the couch, plopping down hard. "It wasn't always. My first year I had no clue." That first year I was buried in residency, I barely knew what day of the week it was. "Dad sent me a present. It said do not open until the anniversary date of my graduation. At the time, I had no idea what the date was. He didn't say a word, and all week I counted down until the day arrived. I ripped open the box, and it was a teddy bear with a stethoscope." I can't help the smile from spreading on my face. "Every year since the week before the anniversary, I'd receive another bear. I thought it would stop after I completed my residency, but it didn't."

I pop to my feet and step toward my home office. I push open the door and wave Brayton in. A wide desk and credenza line one wall, and on the other is a floor-to-ceiling glass bookcase. Running high across all four walls are custom-built wooden shelves. Along each wall sitting on the shelves sit the stethoscope bears, eleven in total. Next to each is a tiny silver medal with the year. Brayton steps to the center of my home office, spinning as he takes in the bears. He pauses when he spots the medal with the current year on it and no bear next to it.

"Wow." Brayton hops up on his tiptoes and reaches high, pulling down one of the bears and fingering the stethoscope. A smile pulls on his face, and he pauses in appreciation. "What a thoughtful gift." He puts the bear back and turns to me. "You're concerned he's not sending one this year?"

I nod. "I've been a terrible daughter this past year. I didn't take his firing very well. Every time we get together or speak on the phone, I somehow work it into the conversation, and we end up arguing. I don't deserve a bear... Does it make me a horrible person because I still want one?"

Brayton wraps me in his arms and leads me out of the office. We plunk down on the couch together, and he presses his lips to the top of my head. "Give him time. I'm sure the bear is on its way. One thing has nothing to do with the other. He sounds like a proud father, and I can see why. You deserve all the recognition in the world."

Brayton must sense my anxiety because he piles on. "Trust me. Your dad has started an important tradition. They're important, they carry meaning, and they help families mark the passage of time, to show their love, to show what they value. It's a beautiful, heartfelt gesture for a beautiful woman. I guarantee you that bear is on its way."

Brayton speaks the words with a confidence I don't feel. He's never met my father, never even heard of him until I brought him up, yet he has more faith in him than I do.

I really am a horrible daughter.

***

Our evening last night was quiet. After lying on the couch with my head on his shoulder, Brayton had me lie flat, and he gave me an over-the-clothes massage. After the emotional journey we both had been on, we avoided turning it into a sensual one. I appreciated the care and time he put in, as he spent nearly ninety minutes exploring every part of my body. I nearly fell asleep on the couch, not recalling ever being so relaxed.

I barely recall Brayton lifting me, carrying me to my bed. Soft whispers in my ear as treated me with so much care. I felt like a princess as he undressed me and climbed in the bed next to me. "Rest beautiful, everything is going to be all right," he whispered affirmations into my ear until I drifted to sleep. At the time, I had no clue how badly I needed that simple gesture, wrapped in the protective cocoon of his arms.

Brayton walks me back to the hospital—another simple gesture that makes me feel things I haven't expected. Each morning, I've passed couples leaving my building together—hand in hand, a shared inside joke, a flirtatious smile to get their partner through the day, a hurried kiss goodbye. Today, I feel like a member of that tribe. My eyes actively seek out others to notice us, to feel envious of us for once, even if it's only for a day.

We approach the hospital, and Brayton reminds me that visiting hours don't start for another two hours. He's going to head to the hotel, hit the gym, shower, and change before returning to sit with Floyd. Not looking to spoil the mood, I don't remind him we expect the results from the steroids tests this morning. We'll all find out soon enough.

Brayton pulls me into one final hug and gives me a lingering kiss that will have to suffice to carry me through the day. "Today is going to be a good day," he whispers before departing.

Once again, he displays a faith I don't carry. I lay my hand on his shoulder, happy to live in this moment and not think about the day ahead. "It already is." My response causes his eyes to sparkle, and I wish we could return to my apartment and end this day with this victory.

My feet remain rooted in place as I watch him disappear toward the garage. Only then do I enter the lobby, my gaze sweeping across the plaques, pausing at my dad's empty spot. Another reminder that even the brightest have faults.

I arrive at my office a half hour before rounds start. The early morning knock on my door doesn't surprise me, but the person standing there does. I rise to my feet. "Dr. Richards." I hear the surprise in my voice. It's always unexpected when the head of the hospital administration shows up at your office unannounced. Dr. Richards sits high up in the administrative tower, rarely venturing down to other units, especially an area as pedestrian as the

Orthopedic Unit. "Good morning. What brings you down to Ortho?"

Dr. Richards is nearly sixty, white, with a full head of matching white hair. He smells of methanol as we shake hands, and I force myself not to react to the smell.

"Morning, Dr. Carmichael. It is my understanding you are consulting with Dr. Morgan on the ballplayer..." His eyes rise as he attempts to recall the name.

"Floyd. Floyd Patterson. Yes, you would be correct." I paint on a plastic smile. Dr. Richards's focus is typically on high-profile cases, schmoozing donors, and working with legal on hospital risk assessment.

"Yes, that's the one. It just came to our attention upstairs this kid is high-profile. I had our media team look into him, and he has over two dozen mentions on sites such as ESPN, and nearly every regional sports publication around. How are things looking?" I feel the judgment in the glare he uses to inspect my office.

"Decent, sir," I begin. "From a medical perspective, nothing serious, just a hairline fracture that will heal on its own. However, Dr. Morgan and I are running a host of tests to understand the underlying cause. He has bone density deterioration."

"Cancer?" he asks.

I shake my head and point to the chair for him to sit. He remains standing. Whatever he came down here for will be over shortly. "That's what we thought initially, but it's been ruled out."

"Family history?"

"Clean, nothing hereditary."

I expect him to continue to drill, but his eyes glaze over. "I'm sure you'll get to the bottom of it, which is why I'm here."

"Sir?" My voice carries the confusion I feel.

"Dr. Carmichael, I just wanted you to know we up in the tower have taken notice of how you operate. You've won a lot of people over, and me, personally, I'm a fan. We receive more detailed reports and administrative waivers from you and your department than anywhere else in the hospital. You have no idea how that translates into saving us on litigation and frivolous lawsuits. I wish your colleagues took the rules as seriously as you do."

A sense of pride feels in my chest. All my work hasn't gone to waste. They've noticed up in the tower, and I am finally getting the respect I've worked so hard for. I can almost hear Brayton's voice in my head. *I told you so.* "Why, thank you, sir. Coming from you, this means a lot."

"Dr. Morgan..." He lowers his chin and gives me a slight head shake. "Brilliant physician, but let's just say his paperwork can be lacking at times." Dr. Richards plants on a conspiracy smile and glares at me.

I steel my face, not giving him a reaction.

"Typically, as you know, for high-profile cases, we have a post-release review with a randomly selected panel of your peers a few weeks after discharge. However, with new budget guidelines, we're reducing this oversight step. We will only be performing panel reviews for a few select cases where we suspect there may be hospital exposure. We haven't communicated this change in policy to anyone in the hospital. Only a handful of trusted, need-to-know doctors will be informed of the change. You are the very first one."

I bite my inner lip, unsure if this change in policy is a good thing or not. "Thank you for letting me know."

"No need to thank me. As you know, in a case such as this, the hospital has stringent reporting guidelines to the appropriate sporting authorities. My understanding is the kid's physician must file a medical report for him to be eligible for the baseball draft. It's a critical legal requirement, and I had a concern until I saw your name listed as the consult. The hospital can't afford sloppy paperwork here. Do you understand?"

I already connect the dots, but I need to hear it from his lips. "Yes, sir. I will consult with Dr. Morgan prior to him submitting the paperwork."

Dr. Richards locks his glare at me, the corner of his eyes tightening as if he's attempting to read me. "I don't think you do. I was the chief administrator on your father's panel. I cast the deciding vote for his dismissal." He bites his lower lip, and I brace for him to take a spit on my office floor. "I still can't believe we had two doctors vote for reprimand and not a dismissal." He lifts his chin in my direction. "Ancient history. I've taken a special interest in your career ever since. I needed to see if the apple fell far from the tree, and let's say I'm impressed. Where your dad was a cowboy, you are a rule follower. Someone the administration can trust. We're making you primary physician for the Patterson kid. We want your signature on that paperwork. We know it will be spotless, like a good little soldier."

I bite my tongue and refuse to respond to his deprecating, backhanded compliment. Dr. Richards has merely confirmed what I've always suspected. I've had a very large target on my back thanks to my dad's actions. I suppress the anger and attempt to focus on what may be an opportunity to step out of his shadow once and for all. I gird my tone. "Is Dr. Morgan aware of this change in the patient assignment?" I must tread carefully. The head of the administration didn't come down to my office to give me a choice. This is a courtesy visit, the decision already made. All I can do is navigate around it.

"I'll leave that to you. I'm sure you're more than capable of handling an ER doctor. You've had years of experience." He smiles, and I take note of his overly bleached white teeth. Yet another dig at the relationship with my father.

I nod like the obedient person I was raised to be, the one who follows the rules. The one who doesn't push back on members of the hierarchy. The one who does as she is told. I want to scream, but I don't. "Not a problem. Is there anything else?"

He laughs. "A future ask. You know our media team is the best in the business. We have to deploy them far too often defensively—they can crush just about anyone with threats of social media blow back and such. I've seen them make grown men cry." A satisfied pride-filled smirk fills his face before he continues. "However, we don't often get a chance to have them spin good news. They'd love if you can convince the ballplayer to talk about his wonderful treatment here at Eastport. I know it's a delicate time with the draft coming up, but you'd get major brownie points if you can connect him with the PR team post draft." Dr. Richards pulls a business card from his pocket. "It's a direct line to the head of the team. I've given him your name and the green light, he said for you to call him anytime. I know you'll use him when the time is right."

I finger the thick cardstock with raised embossed goldleaf ink before cupping it in my palm. "It may be a while, sir."

He nods. "Figured as much." He begins to turn but then pivots back to me with a smile on his crooked face, "I took a look at your patient load before coming down. I see you caught two more broken arms from the Tough Mudder race last weekend. We really should look to sponsor them next fall. They bring us such good business."

For the second time, I clench my teeth to prevent myself from saying something career limiting. Rumor is that Dr. Richards is looking at early retirement in two years. I can hold on that long.

He stuffs a hand in his blazer, and the side of his mouth tips up. "Reach out if Dr. Morgan gives you any trouble." He doesn't try to hide his laugh as he nods and disappears out the doorway.

Only when I know he's gone for sure do I exhale. What the hell just happened? How the hell did all this get dumped in my lap? Just when I was building up trust with Reggie, I have to drop this bombshell on him. Where do I even begin?

My phone pings, and I flip it over. A text from Reggie.

Reggie: I checked on the lab. They are finalizing the results, should have them by ten. Swing by the ER and grab me when you finish your rounds.

There is my answer. I'll need to tell Reggie before he gets the test results. The report that will no longer have his name listed as a physician.

Chapter Fourteen

T he issue with ticking clocks is that sometimes bombs detonate early. "Did you know?" The sharp words attack me from behind as I'm updating a patient chart at the nurses' station.

It's been only thirty minutes since Dr. Richards dropped his bombshell on me, and I've had no time to reach out to Reggie and tiptoe around the news, but from the sound of his voice and veracity of the question, I know it's no longer necessary. He's found out.

I turn toward a steamed Reggie, his enflamed eyes more gray than blue, his arms crossed, and his bottom lip pinched down, his top teeth visible. "I called the lab to confirm the timing of the report, and they said they couldn't provide me that answer. When I asked why, they told me I am no longer listed as the primary physician."

His agitated voice rises, and I notice heads turning in our direction. "Did you have anything to do with it?" He slings an arrow I hadn't expected right into my chest. Just from the question, let alone its tone, I realize Reggie doesn't know me.

My hand rises to my chest. "What? No. How could you..." The Ortho Unit is much more sedate than the ER room where doctors yelling at the top of their lungs is seminormal behavior.

I begin to reach toward Reggie's elbow and am shocked when he takes a step back. Fine. "Follow me." I don't wait for a response, merely leading him back to my office. I wait for the door to close before speaking. "I had nothing to do with this. Why would I—"

"What happened? I'm clueless, yet by the fact that you never asked me what I was talking about, you already knew."

I pump my hands, palms facing the floor. "Dr. Richards—"

"Head of administration Dr. Richards?"

I nod. "Yeah, he was here a little while ago, and he broke the news to me. It was delivered to me as a done deal." My pulse races as I attempt to walk the delicate line all doctors walk when collaborating with another physician. "They want my name on the report since I'm anal about such things. This case is higher profile than I think either of us thought. He mentioned ESPN and a few other names."

"Everybody is watching, Angie. That's the problem. Once people see I was removed as primary physician, they will all begin to question why? What did Dr. Beautiful do to screw this up? The rumors will swirl. This hospital is like high school taken to a whole new level."

I hear his concern, but my mind focuses on only one thing. "Wait, they call you Dr. Beautiful?" I should feel embarrassed about asking him, but I don't.

"Yeah, of course they do." His hands rotate an outline around his face as if he's a Hollywood director framing a shot. "Duh?"

"Ego much?" I joke. All this time, he's been aware of his reputation, and rather than play against type and prove them wrong, he's leaned into it.

"It's not ego when it's true. Besides, I didn't come up with the name. It was bestowed on me, and for once, they got it right." He flicks his wrist toward the ceiling as if the name doesn't mean a thing. "How do you not know this? Why do you think half the staff is chasing after me? Why I feel I have to flirt with the other half? I have to work hard to maintain this name. It could be so much worse.

"Dr. Valdez is called Dr. Jerk because of his lack of bedside manner. He's been bending over backwards and overcompensating for the last few months, but his name has stuck."

I shake my head in disbelief. "And who is this all-powerful *they*? The hidden figures that come up with these names."

Reggie leans against the back of the door. He shrugs. "No one directly knows. I suspect it comes from the hospital administration staff. They are one of the few who cross paths with every department. These nicknames hit every area of the hospital, not just the ER."

I should know better, but I can't stop myself. "Including Ortho?"

A smirk appears on his face, and I'm sure his mind races ahead of mine. "Oh, is someone interested in their nickname?"

He's enjoying this too much. "You know what? Never mind, let's get back to..."

"Hold up a minute." He lifts his hand toward me. "Not so quick, Dr. Cutie."

It's just as I feared. This juvenile game has ranked us based on our physical characteristics. I doubt these names have come from the administration staff. These names reek of a male-dominated section of the hospital, probably finance. "I hold three degrees and more certifications than I can recall, and they have the audacity to call me..."

"Hold your horses." Reggie's smirk grows, and he tilts his head and tries to cover his laugh. "I was just kidding."

I bite my lower lip, upset I fell for his transparent game.

"I got it confused with what I call you in my head."

And bam, we're right back to him flirting with me. Has he not heard a word I've said? No woman wants to only be seen for their physical characteristics. Reggie may be a few years my senior, but he still has a lot of growing up to do.

I glare at him, hoping he can see his response doesn't improve upon the situation.

"It's just a silly name. You should relax and embrace it like I do. And for the record, I know about your three degrees and the certifications you can't recall. You think I just have any old doctor consult with me?" He looks over the tip of his nose and winks at me. "Let alone get me to leave the ER floor."

"We good?" I attempt to pivot us back to the reason he came up here in the first place. "You know about our patient situation?"

He shrugs. "You didn't create it. I'll have to find a way to deal with it. Take me out to dinner, and we'll call it even."

Even in our darkest moments, this man is relentless. A part of me is flattered at how hard he pursues. "Do you really want to go to dinner with me, or are you just trying to rack up brownie points to keep your nickname?" My question is a pure joke, but the flat expression on Reggie's face tells me he's heard differently.

"Out there"—he jerks his neck toward the hospital floor—"I may perform, kid, and joke, Angie, but when it's just the two of us, I always mean what I say. I know you have your doubts about me, but if you ever gave me a chance, you'll see my interest in you is genuine. I admire everything you've accomplished and am in awe of all the things you will accomplish and pray I am close enough to you to see it all occur. You are a special individual who does something most of us only aspire to do—make the world a better place."

My body freezes, chilled by the heartfelt words of a man I had no clue even noticed. This is the second time in a number of days someone who I respect has expressed a confidence in me that I've been struggling for the world to acknowledge.

Over the last eight months, with his constant flirting, I've never once considered Reggie a partner. Even with him opening up, it doesn't change a thing, and I have to make sure we're clear. "Thank you for those kind words, Reggie. I'm impressed by your skill as well. I know how insanely crazy things are in the ER, and you do a wonderful job."

"I hear a but coming." He braces for the inevitable.

"You are a respected colleague, Reggie. We work together."

"Oh, here we go with your rule again."

I shake my head. "Yes, I have a rule, but I want to be perfectly clear because underneath all that bravado, I know you are a nice guy. We are friends. Even if I didn't have the rule, that's all we would ever be. I hope that's enough for you. We good?" I ask him for the second time, and for the second time, he gives me his standard reply.

"I'll have to find a way." He shrugs again. "The lab will ping you when the report is ready. Come down to the ER when they do."

"Of course," I exhale. He begins to turn, and I stop him. "Reggie?" He turns with a curious look on his face. I clear my throat, not sure why I feel an overwhelming need to ask the question. "What is my nickname?"

"You have probably the best nickname in the entire hospital. One every other doctor wished their colleagues saw in them." He pauses, a sense of pride stretching across his face. "Dr. Fix-It." A look of melancholy spreads across his face before he disappears.

I remain locked in place and contemplate the name. My lips pull up into a broad grin. All this time, I've feared the mistakes of my father had tainted my reputation. All this time here, I've worked harder, done more, kept my head down, and had no clue if any of it was being appreciated. The world was watching all along.

I let the nickname sit for a minute. I let my mind marinade with all the different levels of appreciation that come with such a distinguished name at a prestigious hospital. No way this moniker came from Finance, it could only originate from the administration unit. They work everyday with with world-class doctors from throughout the region and understand the challenges and skills required of the doctors on the ground floor. I am truly honored. .

My prideful chest puffs out, and I imagine this must be what Reggie experienced when he became aware of his nickname. I had no clue, and I have him to thank for bringing it to my attention. I've been wrong all this time about how the world was looking at me.

First Brayton, then Dr. Richards, Reggie, and now the hospital staff all stating each in their own way that I am worthy. I am valued. I am viewed with respect.

Maybe I've finally stepped out of my father's shadow once and for all. I feel like I can do anything.

Of course I can, for I am Dr. Fix-It.

Chapter Fifteen

The alert from the lab buzzes on my phone, and I swipe at the hospital iPad and see the report in my inbox. It takes everything in me not to tap it open and get a peek. I owe Reggie the courtesy of waiting until we are together to open it. As far as I'm concerned, the change in primary physician is purely an administrative one. Floyd came into the ER and was assigned to Reggie. Only out of professional courtesy and a bit of curiosity did Reggie pull me in.

iPad in hand, I exit my office and inform the head nurse. Two minutes later, I tap on the frame of an ER patient room, making my presence known.

Reggie twists and nods in my direction before turning his attention back to a patient. It's a middle-aged woman, a deep gash across her forehead, her neck still in the yellow cervical collar that was placed on her in the field by the ambulance unit. Out of habit, I scan her extremities, looking for a possible broken limb and a future client upstairs. I come up empty.

"Stitch up that head wound, send her for a CT head scan, and order up two more chest X-rays. I want to confirm that there isn't any internal damage," Reggie orders the team around him before addressing the lady. "Mrs. Woodson, your husband is on the way. Preliminary exam looks good. We're going to get you cleaned up and check your neck to confirm no injury there. You're a very lucky young lady." His reassuring words elicit a smile from the nervous woman.

Reggie is an excellent physician. Smart, attentive, knowledgeable, and good with people. It's nice to be reminded of this fact as I'm mainly exposed to his over-the-top, flirtatious persona.

He rips off his exam gloves, dropping them in the receptacle, and places his hand under the hand sanitizer dispenser before stepping toward me. "The report's in?"

I nod and follow him out of the room toward the doctors' lounge. We enter, and he gestures for me to take the couch. He slips in next to me. I lift the iPad, and he places his hand on it.

"Before you open the report, I have just one question for you. It will be my last one on the topic, promise."

I brace, expecting his green monster to appear. "Okay," I squeak out.

"When Dr. Richards came to you, did you even consider telling him no? That you wouldn't do it?"

I freeze as guilt runs through my veins. The thought never occurred to me. When a senior hospital administrator, let alone the top administrator, comes to you and makes a personal plea, you do it. You follow the rules.

My silence feeds his annoyance. "I thought so. If this situation were reversed, do you know what I would have done? I would have told him where to stick it. If he has a problem with another doctor, don't you think they deserve the courtesy to be told it to their face?" My gaze lowers to his chest, seeking an escape.

He doesn't wait for me to respond, for there is no response. I want to tell him he's right. I want to tell him so many things, but that opportunity passed hours ago upstairs. That would have been the time to be righteous and brave.

"Let's get on with it. Let's see the report—that is, unless you've already read it." Anger continues to roll off him in waves, and I don't blame him.

I lift the iPad. "No, of course not." My weak words barely reach him as I swipe open the attachment. I angle the iPad so he can see what I see.

I swipe the first two pages and stop. We both speak at the same time. "No traces of steroids of any kind." I take a deep exhale. Brayton is vindicated. My fingers swipe as we scan the details of the test. The lab ran the tests three times with two different teams, an additional step Reggie had ordered. I pinch my brow and point to this unusual request.

"I wanted to make sure. A false positive would've ruined their lives," Reggie whispers, not understanding the magnitude of his words. As much as he comes across as cavalier, he is a deeply caring and committed professional. The administration isn't the only one who misreads him.

"I guess this is good news, in a way." I hear the conflict in my words. Brayton is a man of his word, and I feel like an idiot for doubting him. But it now leaves us with an even bigger medical mystery.

"Steroids would have been the easy way out," Reggie says, pushing back onto the sofa, phone in hand. "The report does highlight a few additional markers which may prove useful, but other than that, nothing we didn't already know. What the hell is going on?"

I turn to face Reggie. "We are missing something. I just don't have a clue what it is." I think back to the hours of research. Did I eliminate something too soon? "I'm going to have to go over all my notes again."

Reggie flips his phone over and begins to swipe.

"You got a thought?" I ask.

He doesn't turn, merely shooting me a sideways glance. "Not me, but I know someone who might."

"That's great. Who?"

"You may not be happy once I tell you who." He half twists toward me, his brows raised.

I suspect already but must hear it from his lips. "Who, Reggie?"

"Your dad." His hands rise in protest before I can react. "He's the smartest doctor I've ever worked with. These medical mysteries are right up his alley."

I feel the weight of my head shaking hard side to side, so hard I fear I'm going to have a headache later. "No, no, no." Of all the names for him to speak. "It's against so many rules, Reggie, you know that."

"No one has to know, Angie," he pleads.

"We'll know." I huff out a loud breath. "That may not bother you one bit, but it will for me. He's no longer associated with the hospital. He doesn't even have a medical license." The more I think about it, the worse it seems. "Oh, and then there is the whole HIPAA privacy law. We could both lose our licenses."

"They'll never find out."

"Said every inmate in prison," I spit back.

He stands, his hands on his hip, shoulders pinned back. "It's a small risk for a patient that is running out of time and options, Angie. This is why we became doctors—to explore every option to save our patient."

My lips purse tight. He's not hearing me. "Every available *legal* option, Doctor." How does he not see what is as clear as the sun in the sky? We are in a heavily regulated and monitored profession and need to act professionally. "We're not doing that, are we clear?"

"So much for the democracy," he mutters underneath his breath.

I rise, my gaze meeting his. "You know it's not like that. I'm open to discussing ..." When his gaze doesn't soften, I add, "... within reason."

His index finger grazes the back of my hand. "Our patient is running out of time. The next time he steps out of bed to use the bathroom, he could snap a bone. The next time he lifts a fork to his mouth, he could fracture his jawbone. Unless we get to the bottom of things soon, it won't be just his career in jeopardy."

He's not being overly dramatic; it's the truth. A hairline fracture may be a best-case scenario for Floyd's future. With the bones deteriorating, it's only a matter of time. Time we don't have. "We go back to the drawing board and start over. Do you want to inform Brayton and Floyd they are steroid-free?" I ask.

He shakes his head. "Why don't you take the point on that. I think he'd prefer to hear it from you rather than me. Besides, I'll get a jump on the research. I want to explore these additional markers in the report. Can you add me to the security release for the file?"

He asks it without a trace of anger, the security release another slight thrown in his direction. "I'm sorry about all of this, Reggie. How about I take you out for a drink when this is all over. Colleague to colleague."

He pauses for a moment before rising off the couch. "I'd like that. And for Floyd's sake, I hope that drink comes soon."

We both exit the lounge, Reggie directly to the nurses' station, and I head to the elevator to update Floyd. He's right—we are going to need to move fast. The baseball draft is next month, and the window to find and fix Floyd is closing quickly.

Chapter Sixteen

B rayton hops to his feet the moment I enter the hospital room, a baseball magazine falling from his lap to the floor. Floyd has earbuds in, lost in his phone.

"Good morning." Brayton steals a quick glance at Floyd before leaning closer and whispering, "Beautiful." He takes a step back as Floyd notices me and whips off his earbuds. "Do you have news for us?"

He's like a happy puppy, overjoyed with his returning owner looking for a treat. "Yes and no," I begin and step toward the bed. Brayton mirrors my motion on the opposite side. "Dr. Morgan and I just reviewed the findings from the latest test, and we're happy to report that there is no sign of steroid use."

I'm not sure what reaction I expected—maybe relief. But neither one of them reacts. They stare at me, expecting more, as if the report findings have no bearing on anything. And it clicks—from their perspective, it doesn't. They told us the test was a waste of time. All we've done is proven that they are men of their words. Nothing more. And in the process, we have wasted a day we could have been exploring other options.

My silence finally causes a reaction. "Is that it?" Floyd asks. It's the first time he's exhibited any frustration. "We told you I don't take steroids or anything like that. I never would." He twists toward his father. "Dad? Can we get out of here? I'm tired of being cooped up in this room."

I jump in. "We're investigating further, following up on a few other leads. We will get to the bottom of this," I say with a confidence I shouldn't have.

"How long?" Brayton asks calmly.

I chew on my bottom lip. "I don't know. These things take time."

Brayton shifts toward his son. "Champ, we'll give them two more days, and then we will go home. Is that good?"

Floyd huffs out his cheeks and crosses his arms against his chest. "Whatever? I'm ordering that Marvel movie tonight. I don't care if it costs twenty dollars."

"Whatever you want. Give me a minute." Brayton grips Floyd's ankle and gives it a squeeze before jutting his neck for me to follow him out of the room.

As soon as the door closes, I speak. "I can't promise you an answer in two days," I say.

"I'm sorry, Angie. That's the most I can give you. You heard him. We can't sit around here forever. We can go home, and you guys can continue to investigate. He's seventeen. He's never sat still for this long in his life."

"And that's the concern, Brayton. If you leave here, Floyd's next break may not be a hairline fracture. It could be more serious." I let my words hang in the air, knowing his concern for his son will force him to hear them. "It sounds to me like he's just bored. Why don't you have some of the kids from the team come visit him. I'm sure that'll lift his spirits."

Brayton shakes his head. "No, we can't do that. We can't tell the other kids. It'll be all over social media before they leave the hospital. Even if Floyd leaves the hospital with a clean bill of health, the news of him in the hospital this close to the draft will scare off enough teams he would drop out the first round or worse, not get drafted at all."

"Wow, I didn't know." There is so much I don't know about amateur sports in this country. I do know that if Floyd is not drafted in the top slots, chances are there won't be any bonus money, and everything their family has worked for will be gone.

"We'll find a way," I whisper to him.

Brayton nods. "I trust you, Angie. And I will take you at your word."

I nod and turn away from him. Did I just give my word, knowing I have no control of this outcome? Worse still is that I gave my word to a man who places his entire belief on a person keeping their word?

What did I just do?

***

Time loses its meaning, and I go into the zone. My dad once described it as a tele-dimensional gateway where the laws of physics and reality don't exist. A doctor becomes so focused they forget to eat, they don't sleep, they don't go to the bathroom, they don't do anything that may jeopardize the research in front of them.

My longest zone was just over eleven hours five years ago. I was preparing to assist on a tricky operation of a patient that was triple-jointed. I had to research the unusual procedure that is performed less than twenty times a year anywhere in the world. My research didn't stop until I could visualize every step of the procedure in my head over and over. It proved successful, and I crashed and slept for two days after the operation.

I'm merely six hours into my research when a knock on my door disturbs me. I look up to find Reggie.

"It's nearly seven. I'm headed home to continue my research. Wanted to check to see if you've come up with anything yet." Reggie is dressed in tan slacks and a navy polo shirt, backpack slung across his shoulder.

I raise a pencil in his direction and tap the notepad on the top of my desk. "Chasing down a few leads. I thought I had it earlier but had to rule it out because Floyd isn't a Caucasian woman over the age of forty living in a Nordic country."

"Ahh, Fintopalidia syndrome. I crossed that off the list this morning." He shoots me a tired smile and pushes off from the doorway. "I know this may be a crazy idea, but do you want to come over tonight, spend the night?" He takes a step toward me. "As colleagues. We could research in the same space. This way, as we eliminate things, we can tell the other and eliminate duplication."

I pause. I had considered this approach this morning and ruled it out. Not because of Reggie, but because of science. "It sounds appealing, Reggie, it really does. But in my gut, I feel like I've missed something. From a scientific protocol perspective, this approach makes sense. With this approach, if one of us misses something, the other one should catch it. The chances of both of us missing the same element separately are much lower than if we looked at things together."

He shrugs his shoulder, fatigue in his movement. He's too tired to argue with me. "I tried. You have my address and number if you change your mind."

I shoot a soft smile at him. "You have the same for me. I don't care what time it is."

He nods before waving. "Good night and happy hunting."

***

It doesn't take me long to get back into the zone. It feels like only minutes before I hear another knock on the door, but when I peek up and see the darkness outside, I know it's been a few hours.

Brayton is standing in my doorway with a large plastic bag in one hand. "I thought I'd find you here," he says, lifting the bag. "I checked with Chef Marian after visiting hours, and she mentioned she hadn't heard from you tonight." Brayton stands behind my guest chair. "I hope you don't mind I took the liberty of having her prepare us dinner."

"Us?" I question and scratch my scalp with the end of the pencil. "I'm kind of in the middle of something, Brayton." I point to the mess of my desk.

"I know," he says, stepping around the chair. "And I knew you probably hadn't eaten all day. It looks like you still have several hours ahead of you, and it's already nine thirty in the evening. Let me take you home. You take five minutes to eat, and I'll stay with you while you finish your research."

His offer sounds incredible, and it is the sweetest. But I know how I get when I'm in the zone. "I'm horrible company when I get this way."

"Good because there is a documentary on Netflix I'd been meaning to watch." He shoots me that sexy smirk, and I know I can't say no to the man that has somehow wormed his way into my heart. "I just want to make sure you are safe, eat a little something, and get at least six hours of sleep."

I hold up my hand, three fingers pointing back at him.

"Five," he counters.

I hold up four fingers. "Final offer."

"Fine, but we leave now while this food is still warm. After that meal last night, I'll never say a bad word about hospital food ever again."

His response draws a dry laugh from me. "Good to see you coming around to my ways." I begin to gather the papers on the desk as he steps back.

"You have no idea how much of an influence you've been on me, Angie."

I try not to react to his declaration. I can't tell him how much he's affected me in such a short time. None of it will matter if we can't solve the problem plaguing his son.

Chapter Seventeen

T rue to his word, after watching me eat half a meal, Brayton leaves me alone to research. Although I have a home office, I much prefer to spread out on the large couch and table in the living room. As a result, Brayton sequesters himself in the bedroom. He's formed an online watch party with Floyd, and they co-streamed some baseball documentary I've never heard of. The two of them stay on the phone as they watched together, a running commentary.

It is the most adorable thing I've ever seen and only provides more motivation for me to solve this mystery.

I quickly lose track of time again as the voices disappear and the lights turn off behind my closed bedroom door. A ping on my phone breaks my concentration, and I flip it over.

That can't be right. The phone informs me it is three thirty-six in the morning. A text from Reggie.

Reggie: I got news and am on my way. Let the doorman know to let me up. Will be there in five.

It's not until I move that I feel my body protest the hours of being slumped over writing on a table meant for coffee, not writing.

Me: Will do, I'll crack the door. Come right in when you arrive.

I quickly call down to the lobby and let Wilton know about my early morning visitor and then crack open the front door. I stumble into the bathroom and stare at a woman I barely recognize. My hair is strung out, and red streaks of lightning bolts race across my eyes, giving away the number of hours I've stared at a screen. My neck is stiff, and my lower back aches from slumping over on the couch. I'm a mess. What a sight for a man known as Dr. Beautiful to see. I splash water across my face and run a wide comb through my hair, attempting to give it some shape. It's pointless.

My feet turn at the sound of a knock on the door, followed by the squeak of it opening. I exit the bathroom and spot an equally disoriented Reggie standing in my living room. I wave him over to the couch, and he plasters a smile on his face as wide as I've ever seen. He's holding up a three-by-five canary index card and pushes it in my direction.

Analiegh-Bradley Syndrome is neatly printed on the card in bold black lettering. A definitive diagnosis.

The name only feels vaguely familiar. I'm sure it is referenced in one of the dozens of medical books I've been poring over.

"Is this..." I don't complete my thought, instead choosing to flip to my laptop and log back onto the hospital's online reference library. I type in the name on the search bar, and only three links are returned. As suspected, it's a rare disease.

A wide yawn escapes from my lips as I wipe my eyes and click. Analiegh-Bradley syndrome is a rare disease usually associated with people over the age of forty. Less than one hundred thousand cases have been reported in the world over the last twenty years. As I scan the list of symptoms, it's a near perfect match for what Floyd is experiencing, Loss of bone density, hairline fractures, tingling sensation at the extremities, increased fatigue, and thirst. There is no definite conclusion as to the cause of the disease, only that it is linked to the autoimmune system and kidneys. Scientists haven't been able to determine whether it is a germ or a virus. I skip the thirty screens of research and skim ahead to the treatment options.

My fingers fly across the screen, and I take in the good news. Finally. All of a doctor's favorite words are there: curable, treatable, fast recovery, no long-lasting effects. A patient can expect to return to a normal life. I hop to my feet with a wide grin, ready to celebrate, when my eyes continue to scan for treatment.

It's a drug cocktail of readily accessible, fast-acting drugs. Very few side effects. The problem isn't in the accessibility of the drugs, it's in the composition of the drugs. One drug in particular—dexamethasone. It's a powerful and required part of the drug cocktail.

It is also a steroid.

"I see you discovered the dilemma." The sound of his voice catches me by surprise. My lack of sleep had me already forgetting Reggie was standing two feet from me.

Reggie is wearing a gray Eastport General T-shirt and matching gym shorts. I have a matching pair, part of our *Welcome to Eastport* care package every doctor receives for the year-end holiday season. Reggie must've come straight to my place without a thought of changing on his mind.

I turn back to the laptop and continue to scan.

"There is no other option. All treatment plans lead back to dexamethasone." He's reading my mind. There has to be another option.

I close the laptop and twist to face him. "He has to take the steroid to get better," I speak out loud, stating the obvious.

"And if he does, it means his medical report will be flagged, making him ineligible for the draft. Which means the end of his baseball career before it even gets started." Reggie has had more time to put together the pieces, his conclusion ahead of where my mind was racing. But he's right.

If we treat him, he gets better but will be ineligible for the draft. If we don't treat him, he doesn't get better, probably suffers more breaks, and will be ineligible for the draft.

"There has to be an exception. Some medical exemption. Dexamethasone isn't a performance-enhancing drug. Surely they've accounted for these scenarios in their policies." I'm rambling, not expecting Reggie to have a response.

He surprises me. "I've begun to check, and yes, there are a handful of exceptions."

"Yes, I knew it." I rise and take a step toward him.

He raises a hand. "Not so fast. There are only four diseases on the exception list, and as you can guess, Analiegh-Bradley syndrome isn't one of them."

"We'll just have to get it added to the list." I wave a hand, deceiving myself that it could be this simple.

Reggie takes a step back, crossing his arms, a look of defeat on his face, "You are more than welcome to take a crack at it. Over the last hour, I've looked into the process, and it is lengthy, it is slow, and it requires a committee review and vote. There are currently six other diseases under review. The oldest one is coming up on two years."

"Floyd doesn't have two years to wait." As much as I know about sports-related injuries, I know very little about sports themselves, let alone amateur sports. All I do know is the urgency in Brayton's voice whenever he mentioned the upcoming baseball draft. "Damn bureaucracy!" I shout out to no one.

Reggie mocks me with a chuckle. "Rules." He shakes a fist toward the sky. "I smite thee."

"Are you making fun of me right now? I'm in no condition to hear your jokes." My words roll off him, and it's not lost on me the irony—the queen of rules voicing frustration with a process.

"I just find it humorous. We'll need to test Floyd to confirm he has the syndrome, now that we know what we are looking for, but after that, it becomes a tough call. Thank god I'm not the doctor of record on this one." He says the line with a slight smirk and no humor in his voice.

He's right. This is a high-profile case, and even though Dr. Richards shared with me that it won't be up for a review panel, there still will be filings required. His discharge papers and the official medical report to the baseball league for the draft. Both will need to mention not only the diagnosis but also the treatment plan.

"How are you going to handle this?" And he freezes, a strange look I can't place sweeping across his face. I assume for a moment it's because he understands the gravity of the situation. But then I notice his gaze is not directed at me, but over my shoulder.

I don't need to turn to know what he is staring at, but the deep scratchy voice behind me provides the answer. "Good morning, Dr. Morgan."

Brayton.

Chapter Eighteen

R eggie's eyes shut tight for a breath before he reopens them. He's not seeing an illusion; it is Brayton coming out of my bedroom wearing nothing but a pair of boxer shorts. Nothing I can say will change this fact.

"Good morning, Mr. Patterson," Reggie says with a pinched brow, his gaze returning to me with a *you've got to be shitting me* expression.

Reggie backs up slowly. Brayton appears next to me. "Sorry to disturb you, Dr. Carmichael. I'll see you back at the hospital," he says, and I remain speechless. "I guess when you told me you'd be up all night playing doctor, you were serious." He scrunches his face at me before turning and giving me his back.

It is Brayton who follows him to the door. I'm too stunned to hear what they whisper before Brayton locks the door and takes me by the hand, leading me back to the bedroom.

"Come, you need rest," he says as I climb into the bed. He pulls the sheet and comforter up over me and leans over and places a kiss on my forehead. "Dr. Morgan said you are getting close. He said you guys want to run an additional test on Floyd this morning, and if what you suspect is proven, there may be a path forward. Is it true?"

Brayton looks down at me with a look of hope I hate to douse. Reggie has only given him the broad strokes. Like most art, the devil is in the details. "Can you tell me again when the draft is?"

Brayton strokes my head, and I close my eyes. It feels so damn good. "Next month, in about four weeks."

"What if we find a way to get Floyd healthy but it's not in time for the draft? What happens then? Does he just apply

for the next one in a few months?" I really need to find time
to research the details behind the baseball draft.

Brayton stops stroking my hair. "What aren't you telling
me?" His voice fills with concern.

"Nothing yet. I'm just trying to understand the timeline.
What options are there if he's not ready for the draft? He'll
just roll onto the next one, right?" I brace and pray it's that
simple.

"For the average high school player, yeah, they apply for
the next draft, but it's a year out," Brayton clarifies.

I nod. "Floyd will still only be eighteen. That's not bad."

"It would be disastrous." Brayton's voice carries an urgent
grip of panic. "Floyd isn't your average high school kid. He's
already declared for the draft and should go first round.
Once you do that, you can't drop out of the draft. Everyone
is watching, teams are positioning and planning based on
who's applied. For a top prospect to pull out this close to the
draft is like flashing a warning light into the night sky. Every
club will investigate to see why, regardless of the reason
we give in a press release. Just the hint of the word 'injury'
will have teams bailing. First round becomes a pipe dream.
Hell, he'd be lucky to be drafted at all. Without a first-round
pick, there goes the signing bonus and everything else
attached to it."

I rack my brain for a solution that could work. "What
about college? Couldn't Floyd go to college and play ball
until the next draft?"

Once again, Brayton shakes his head. "If we opt for
college, it's a four-year commitment. He wouldn't be
eligible to be drafted until he is twenty-one."

"Is that so bad?" I don't know if it's the fatigue or my lack
of understanding of sports that makes it hard for me to not
see this as an option.

"The problem is we stated our intention to be in the
draft. Same problem. If we pull out and say we intend
to go the college route, every school is going to take it
as a warning sign and will investigate. There are only a
handful of colleges that provide enough quality training
to make it to the top of the profession. And they have
their pick of prospects. They won't waste a scholarship
on a player who could be injured. Other colleges may

take a flier on Floyd, but they lack the sports program to support the dream of making it all the way. In either case, without a scholarship, we couldn't afford those colleges." I listen intently as Brayton takes his time to explain why the options are limited.

"So, it's all or nothing with Floyd and the draft?" I state the obvious.

Brayton smiles down at me. He's just knocked down every option out there. There's only one path to Floyd's future. The one path I can't deliver to him.

"Why are you smiling? You've just painted a gruesome picture."

Brayton leans over the bed and places a kiss on my lips. "I trust you, Angie. I trust you'll find a way clear for us. And as much as I'm falling hard for you, I am trusting you with something even more precious than my heart. I'm trusting you with my son."

I know later I will replay the mention of him trusting me with his heart on repeat. But in this moment, all I feel is the weight of navigating this impossible path.

He pulls the top of the comforter tight around my neck and places another kiss on my forehead before I can speak. "Get some rest. You promised me you'd get at least four hours of rest. It sounds like you are going to need it. Tomorrow is going to be a special day. I can feel it. Can you?"

Brayton doesn't wait for me to answer. He plops onto the bed next to me and wraps an arm around me. I curl up against his hard chest and try to ignore the sound of my heartbeat. It drums hard against my chest. It's the sound of doom on the horizon. That's what I feel coming.

Chapter Nineteen

I leave my condo early, convincing Brayton to sleep in while I take a walk to the hospital. The cool morning air needed to clear my head and prepare for the day. My head is anything but clear, and the minute I stride up the walkway to the hospital, I know it's about to get muddier.

Reggie leans against one of the hospital columns, coffee in one hand and phone in the other. He spots me and stuffs the phone in his pocket. He's been waiting for me.

"I wasn't sure you were going to come in early..." He glances over my shoulder. "Or alone."

"Good morning to you too," I snap harsher than intended. I can normally get by with as little as four hours of sleep but not when my head refused to settle. Brayton had no issue falling back to sleep, Reggie's appearance at my apartment in the middle of the night barely registering. He read it as two dedicated doctors collaborating. I believe him being my condo and in my bed helped him process it all.

I fear Reggie won't have the same outlook. My lack of sleep and the sense of impending doom has me on edge, and I prepare for the first attack of the day.

"How long have you two been bumping uglies?" he asks, and I take a small step back as if assaulted.

"Excuse me?"

"You heard me. I thought we were in this together." He whips his hand out, flicking the remaining coffee across the walkway behind him. A crimson-brown bloodstain splatter marks the concrete. He then crumbles the paper coffee cup.

"Me and you together? What would give you..." His eyes flash, and I realize my mistake. "I'm sorry, you meant on the case."

Reggie scans the area around us, holding the crumbled cup out. When he doesn't spot a garbage can nearby, he holds it behind his back. "I think you've made yourself perfectly clear about the prospects of that ever happening, Angie. I'm talking about you sleeping with the guardian of our patient. Doesn't this violate one of your precious rules?"

I shake my head. "What I do in my personal life—"

"I don't give a flying fuck about your personal life, Angie. What I care about is a colleague I trusted didn't come clean with a vital piece of information that could impact the care of my... our... fuck it, your patient." I hear the frustration in his voice and understand the hurt.

"It's not an issue," I mutter, not even convincing myself.

Reggie doesn't back down. "Like hell it's not. If you aren't having undue influence over him, then he may have influence over you, which is all I care about. I thought you were smarter than that."

His last line snaps like a whip across my backside, stinging and blinding me momentarily. I scoff. "That's rich coming from a man who flaunts rules on a regular basis. As if it's any of your concern, whatever goes on between Brayton and I will not impact the care or decisions I make about his son."

Our gazes lock, and Reggie holds it for a few beats. He waits for me to expand on my statement, and when he realizes I won't waver, his shoulders drop. "Fine. That's all I needed to hear."

He turns toward the entrance to the hospital, and I follow. "With your permission, since you are now the official physician on record, I'd like to order up the tests to confirm the Analiegh-Bradley syndrome this morning. We'll need to draw more blood and obtain a sample from his kidney. Am I okay to proceed?"

Reggie's mood shifts with the wind. One moment he's all alpha ready to chew my head off, and the next he's the subservient, dutiful physician asking for permission. I'm getting whiplash trying to keep up.

Rather than try to soothe his bruised ego, I ignore that part of his statement. "Go right ahead. You'll get pinged when the results are ready. I updated your access to the file as well. From now on, you'll see everything I see."

He nods as we cross the lobby. My gaze, as always, scans toward the plaques. "Just call him. He'd be happy to hear from you," Reggie says over my shoulder.

Another person realizing what I'm looking at. How many people in the hospital know? I shake my head. "I wish it was that easy. Every time we talk it always spirals into screams."

Reggie's reaction surprises me. He laughs. "I never knew your dad to be much of a screamer, so I'm assuming you mean each time it's you who winds up screaming?"

I process his words and realize he's right. My dad has remained calm. Calm about his actions, confident he's done the right thing. Nonchalant about the impact his decision has had. Of course, it's enough to make me scream.

"Go prep our patient." I'm not sure I can spare the energy to speak with Dad today. I'm already exhausted, and the day has yet to begin. "I'm not sure today is the best day for me to call him. We have a lot going on."

Reggie halts by the elevator bank without pressing a button. "Well, if you do speak to him, thank him for the consult last night, but tell him it took me twenty minutes to locate a yellow index card."

"Last night? Wait... You didn't..." The tension returns to my body, and I feel my blood pressure rising. For a moment last evening when Reggie handed me the yellow card, I thought it odd. The same type of card dad would place on my dresser when I was stumped playing the medical mystery game with him. I was too tired last night to make the connection. It's so obvious now.

He lifts his hands toward me. "Like I've told you, your dad is the smartest doctor I've ever had the pleasure of working with. We were running out of time and dead ends. It was him who pointed me toward Analiegh-Bradley syndrome. He has thirty-plus years of experience. He's seen more than either of us combined."

"Even after you and I spoke about how you wouldn't do that?"

"We spoke about a lot of things, like not sleeping with the person who makes medical decisions for our underage patient."

All I hear is jealousy in his voice, but I know he believes it's different. I would never compromise the care of a patient. Reggie must know that. How could he not? "What I'm doing isn't illegal. What you did may very well be. Dad doesn't work here; he doesn't have a medical license..." I continue to rail on the ten other reasons why what he did is wrong.

Reggie's jaw clenches, frustration written across his face. "Your dad is a professional. You should know that. No names were shared. I don't understand why you are so upset? If I hadn't called him, we'd still be banging our heads against the wall. Cut your dad a break, for once."

I press the elevator call button to escape. I've heard enough. And now, because of Reggie's action, I must call my dad to see how far Reggie pushed the envelope. The elevator dings, and I spit in Reggie's direction, "I'll give him a call, and he'd better verify everything you've just said, or there will be hell to pay."

Reggie doesn't respond, merely letting silence and his anger respond for him. I step onto the elevator and mash the button to the Ortho Unit.

I look out of the elevator and am perplexed to find Reggie still standing outside the elevator. "Are you coming?"

His eyes tighten, and he looks at me as if it's the most ridiculous thing he's ever heard. "I'll wait for the next one."

I don't argue, I don't respond, I don't move. Our eyes remain locked in a silent war between our opposing views of the world. The door closes shut, and I scream to the ceiling loud enough I'm sure Reggie hears it in the lobby. I don't feel any relief. The demons and stress of the day still hang heavy on my shoulders.

All I've done is prove Reggie right—I am a screamer.

Chapter Twenty

W hen he insisted that we meet in person, I should have said no. That was the first warning sign I ignored. When he convinced me he'll make it easy and meet me at the hospital, my brain was too much in a fog to realize how terrible an idea it was at the time.

Yet, here I am, having just returned to my office after completing my rounds, and a familiar profile greets me. His back is to the door, his left leg crossed over his knee, sitting in my guest chair, a medical magazine in his hand as if he has all the time in the world.

I pause and let the disbelief flow through me. My dad is here. In the hospital he was fired from. In the building he was escorted from by security. In my office, not his. Sitting in my guest chair. Everything about this feels awkward and wrong, and the minute I let my presence be known, I know it will only get worse.

I clear my throat, bringing his attention to me, and enter. "Hope I didn't keep you waiting."

He stands. My dad is a handsome man. His sixtieth birthday is in his recent rear view, but you would never guess it. Only a dusting of gray in his short Afro near his temple gives away his age. Clean-shaven, woodsy cologne, and bright dark eyes that lock on you and make you feel as if you are his entire world. Being in the presence of my father always takes me back to my childhood. He was my everyday hero, the person I always wanted to be.

"Not at all. I like what you've done with your office. It actually looks like you spend time here for a change." He pulls me into a hug and gives me a peck on my cheek, a warm smile, and a shoulder squeeze as if this is just another typical day.

My pulse races as I step around the desk and sit. "I hope you didn't have any issues downstairs." I'm rambling, not sure what the policy is for security and ex-employees. I created an all-access pass for him in the system, shot an email to the head of security, and left my cell number. It may have been overkill, but I didn't want an incident nor to violate any rules.

My dad swipes a hand in the air. "Chuck and I go way back. I have an open invitation."

His answer throws me. "Yet today is your first time back since..."

He shifts in the chair, and the discomfort I normally feel when we approach this topic grows. "I was just waiting for an invitation from you... and even when you offered up a meeting, it was me who had to prod you to make it here. I hope I didn't overstep."

"Wait..." My hand flies to my chest. All this time, Dad hasn't been back to the hospital because of me? "I thought you didn't want... that it might bring back too many..."

"Oh please," he scoffs. "I'm not ashamed of what I did or what happened to me. I have no issue looking anyone in this building in the eye." His gaze softens, and he lowers his voice. "I never wanted to make it difficult for you. I figured if I disappeared, everyone would be able to see the shine you've always had."

I bounce out of the chair and hop around the desk and give my dad another hug, this one much tighter, much longer, and more heartfelt. "You have no idea what those words mean to me, Dad."

Water wells in his eyes as I sniffle away my own and return to my chair. "Wow, this is only going to make what I'm about to say even harder." I avoid his gaze and stare at the cheap plastic hospital pen on the top of my desk. "I can't have you talking to Dr. Morgan about patient care." I bite down on my lower lip and brace for the argument.

A chuckle escapes his mouth.

"You find this funny? We can get in a lot of..."

He raises his hand to stop my soliloquy on hospital policy, something I'm extremely good at and something he despises. "That's not it, dear. I'm laughing because I knew he'd tell you. He's been hung up on you ever since he did his residency under me."

"What? You two have been talking about me? For how long? His residency? He didn't even know me then; I was away at college." So many questions race through my head.

A full-on laugh accompanies his reply. "He saw a picture of you on my desk when he started his residency. Asked about you nearly every day for six months. You know how proud of you I've always been. I had no problem mentioning all your exploits. He had it bad for you, and that first time you dropped by the hospital on one of your breaks to visit... Let's just say he didn't shut up for another year.

"I can't believe you haven't noticed by now. The moment he was assigned here, I expected him to show up at your door the next day and ask you out. I'm shocked it took him this long to figure out a way to work with you."

My head spins with my dad's offload. None of this makes sense. Reggie is Reggie, the flirtatious, not-serious doctor who enjoys women tripping over themselves. He's not the type to carry a torch for someone. Let alone someone like me.

"We are and will always only be colleagues, Dad." If Reggie is talking to my dad, I need to put a pin in whatever fantasy the two of them may be sharing. "Besides, I'm seeing someone."

Dad leans forward, a spark of interest in his eyes. "Is this a meet-your-dad type of someone or a pass-the-time someone?"

I can't believe my ears. Has my dad been thinking about my sex life? "It's a 'none of your business, we're figuring it out' type of someone." I need to shift this topic, or I'm going to go to hell. "Can we get back to ..."

"Did Reggie write it on a yellow card for you?" he asks, and I snicker. "It took me a half hour to convince him to do that and deliver it to you in person in the middle of the night. I wanted to have him place it on your dresser."

"Because that wouldn't be creepy at all." I shake my head. "Obviously I'm pleased you were able to give us a diagnosis that has eluded us, but Dad, you can't do that again. It's too risky."

Once again, he laughs at my concern. "I'm guessing Reggie didn't tell you about the contract?"

I scratch my head. "What contract? What are you talking about."

Dad pulls out a dollar bill from his pocket and places it on edge of the desk. "I know how you are with rules and all. So when he called, I sent him a one-page consulting contract for one dollar. It states I don't have an active medical license and am only offering advice. No patient names are provided to me, and I can't disclose any information about the discussion with anyone outside the hospital. I may be cavalier with my career, dear, but I respect you and would never do that to yours."

Reggie is right. I do need to cut my dad a break. He's been through so much in such a short timeframe, and yet he is here to help me and still find a way to stay within rules for my benefit. "I'm sorry, Dad. I didn't mean to ..."

He taps the bill. "You can keep my fee, and we'll call it even." He winks at me the way he used to when I was a kid, and it feels good not to be yelling.

"How's the consulting going?" I ask.

My dad leans back in the chair, a bright smile spreading across his face. "I'm shocked how much I'm enjoying it." His perfect white teeth peek out from beneath the smile. "There are so many clinics and small hospitals that lack the resources of Eastport and large metropolitan hospitals. I swoop in for a week behind the scenes and put together a plan for them to improve the quality of care. Short-term fixes and long-term goals. I've been invited to so many conferences to speak I'm considering putting together a TED Talk."

Being a doctor was all I ever envisioned my dad as. The way he put on his lab coat like a superhero, going off to save lives. He was always beaming, always happy, and I never imagined he'd be satisfied doing anything else. Yet, sitting here and watching him glow, I get a sense for the first time that he's happy. Maybe even happier than before. Now he doesn't have to deal with the heartbreak of working with patients on losing battles.

"No regrets?" I whisper.

"Not a one." He's told me this a thousand times, but today is the first day I hear him. "I know you love your rules, but remember, rules are created by humans who are not perfect. Think of the standard of care—they evolve and change as we learn more, as our tools improve. As doctors, we feel the shift before the playbook gets updated, you know that. Things we were told not to do ten years ago became standard procedure years later, and today no one even questions them. So don't be bound by a rule stuck in the past. You know as the person in the trenches what is right for your patient. Do what is right. The rules will just have to adjust."

"HIPAA is a pretty big rule. I don't see it changing anytime soon." My counter is factual but weak. I'm beginning to understand his logic.

"Yet, it is still just a rule written by a committee. As doctors, we are trained to save lives. And if you come to a point where you must choose your patient's life or comply with an arbitrary rule, I will choose my patient every single time. If I had a nickel for every doctor spoken with at a conference who shook my hand and lament about ridiculous rules they have to deal with on a daily basis, I'd retire. I've told them to take the plunge but most of them still have medical school loans to worry about." Dad snickers at his running commentary.

This is the longest we've discussed his history without screaming, and I have to bring up a painful topic. "They removed your plaque from the lobby." The image of the empty space is too much for me to keep in.

His chuckle warns me I've gotten something else wrong. "Dear, I took that plaque. Or rather, I had a friend in maintenance remove it and give it to me. I worked hard for that award. It's sitting on a shelf in my man cave at home."

"But I thought..."

"It's okay. Most doctors here agreed with my decision at the time. I nearly had enough support on the panel. But you know how it goes. It came down to the pencil pushers and the administrators. Dr. Richards gave the final vote. That man is more concerned with the hospital's bottom

line and not offending anyone than to be brave and bold.
This hospital will be a better place once he retires."

I bristle at the mention of Dr. Richards. The man I've
secretly aligned with. That nagging feeling of being the
Goody Two-shoes returns.

"You broke the rules and have not a shred of regret, do
you?"

His gaze floats over my shoulder toward my degrees
displayed prominently on the wall behind me. "It may
seem like I don't care, but dear, I did agonize over it—lost
a great deal of sleep. But at the end of the day, the path was
clear. There really wasn't a choice." His jaw ticks, and his
gaze softens. "When you are dealing with a patient's future
or in this case their life, things are never black and white. I
pray you are never in that situation, but I know if you are
you'll do the right thing. I have no question about it."

I wish I had my father's cavalier attitude against rules. All
my life, I've been taught to respect them, to follow them.
Shifting my attitude is not something that can happen in a
day, a week, a month, or possibly a lifetime. But my dad is
right about one thing: I've never been in a situation like his.
Everyone has values, but their true beliefs shine through
when those values are put to the test.

I've been a horrible daughter, not believing him, not
supporting him. Berating him even after he lost his job, his
licenses, everything. Yet he is here because I called. Yet he
is here still believing that I will do the right thing.

"I wish it was you who called me last night and not
Reggie." His voice cracks for the first time since I've entered
the room. "I do miss playing the medical detective game
with you as my Dr. Watson."

I giggle at the silly name he gave me when he'd quizzed
me back in medical school. I was Dr. Watson to his Sherlock.
I miss the games too. "I told Reggie not to call you."

A twinkle returns to my dad's eye. "I hope you aren't mad
because he broke your rule. It was the right thing to do.
His approach was off. He was focusing on everything the
patient is and trying to find a disease that fit the profile.
These medical mysteries don't follow rules—you have to
look at them upside down. Once I told him to remove
the patient from the equation, look at the symptoms,

and locate the disease even if it didn't seem like a likely candidate, we narrowed it down pretty quickly."

"Even if it's a disease associated with a forty-year-old patient..."

"Diseases don't play by the rules, so why should you?" It's not the first time he's spoken these words to me.

"Treat the whole patient," I repeat his mantra. Look beyond what is right in front of your face.

Dad nods, the dimple on his right cheek making an appearance for the first time. We both pause and enjoy the silence for a beat.

"I brought you something." He leans forward in his chair and pulls out a large plastic shopping bag that had been placed underneath the edge of my desk. I had been so stunned my dad was in my office I failed to notice this bright pink bag.

He reaches in and pulls out a silver, pink, and blue gift-wrapped box. My hand clutches my chest. He didn't forget.

"You can't open it until your special day, but happy anniversary."

I already picture my bear with the stethoscope on the empty spot at home. My dad hadn't forgotten. He's proven me wrong yet again.

When will I open my eyes and see that my dad is right far more often than I give him credit for? I step around the desk as he rises. I wrap him in a bear hug, burying my face into the crook of his neck.

I feel the wetness on my cheek before I realize I'm crying. "I've missed you. I've missed this. I've missed my dad."

He runs a hand up and down my back. "I've never gone anywhere, dear. I never will."

I squeeze him with all my might, making sure this moment is real. I've taken too long to pick up the phone. I've wasted too much time afraid of doing the wrong thing than focusing on doing the right thing.

No more.

Starting today, I will be brave, I will be fearless, I will be my father's daughter. I will be Doctor Fix-It.

Chapter Twenty-One

I go at it alone.
We've received the test results from the lab confirming Analiegh-Bradley Syndrome, and rather than accompany me to share this possibly life-altering news to the family, I assign Reggie as my dad's personal escort on the Dr. Carmichael returns to Eastport General Hospital world tour. Reggie and Dad have a history, and Reggie doesn't hesitate to rush off with him.

I blink away the exhaustion racing through my body and gird myself with my new attitude to face the Pattersons.

My tentative knock must have been too soft as Brayton hops to his feet with surprise in his eyes as I enter. He stuffs a colorful brochure onto the seat of the chair behind him before stepping toward Floyd's breakfast tray. He removes the straw from the empty apple juice container, pulling my attention toward him.

"Hey, didn't hear you... you look... Do you have news?" His face flashes from surprise to concern in an instant, and I'm sure the puzzled look on my face is only adding to his anxiety.

I nod. "We believe we've isolated the cause of the issues. Dr. Morgan and I are working on treatment options, and right now, the prognosis looks promising. It's possible you can be fully recovered with a completely clean bill of health in a matter of weeks."

Brayton's eyes light up with joy, and he turns to his son, squeezing his ankles and shooting him a smile. "I told you Angie would fix it."

I hear my moniker out of his mouth, and a sense of pride sweeps through me. Their belief and trust is overwhelming.

Trust.

I let the pair complete their celebration before I jerk my neck for Brayton to follow. "When you have a moment, can we talk?"

He's standing by the side of his son's bed, the two of them sharing hugs. It's a beautiful moment which I feel bad tossing a wet blanket across.

"Sure," he says. "Your office in five?"

The office is so clinical. What I need to discuss with him deserves a more intimate setting. I shake my head. "The rooftop. You do remember how to get there, right?"

He blinks at me through happy eyes and smiles and taps his temple. "Wouldn't forget it for the world. A perfect place to celebrate. See you soon."

My weak smile is ignored in his celebration as I step out of the room backward and prepare to meet him on the rooftop and shatter the dream they've been working toward for over half a decade.

***

The squeak of the door doesn't cause me to turn. My gaze is glued to the distant powder puff clouds that have no sense of the impending doom I feel in my chest.

"What a beautiful sight." His words do cause me to turn and face him. His gaze is locked on me, not on the horizon. I've never seen him happier, his beautiful face beaming. So entranced, I fail to notice how quickly he strides toward me, and then his arms are around me, my shoulders arched backward, his lips pressed against mine as if this is a Broadway musical, the audience on their feet applauding the magnificent finale.

I fool myself and pretend this is real for the moment. It may be the last kiss we share after I reveal the truth and destroy the happy bubble he is living in. His strong hand holds the back of my head as his tongue explores every inch of my mouth. He is a passionate man, no longer holding back. His tongue swipes across mine, exploring every part of my mouth as if he's laying claim. He's ready for a celebration, the most important thing in his world back on the righteous path, his focus on our us. If only it was all so simple.

"This is incredible, Angie. You've saved my son. Saved me. I knew you would. There is so much we have to talk about." We finally straighten up, yet he continues to run his fingertips across my cheeks, our noses inches away from each other. "There's so much more I have to say..."

Brayton is expecting the final curtain to fall, the happily ever after. As a doctor, I know not everyone gets the happy ending. I must break the news to him that this isn't the end of the play but is the twist in the final act. "Me too."

I take a step back and turn toward the edge of the roof. I sense Brayton shadowing my movement behind me. I turn to face him. "It's about the treatment for Floyd."

Concern sweeps his face. "I thought you said..."

"I know." I cut him off before he falls down that rabbit hole. "Floyd has a rare bone disease called Analiegh-Bradley syndrome. There are less than a hundred recorded cases worldwide and almost none of them as young as Floyd. That's why we were initially stumped, but the tests we've run this morning confirmed the diagnosis."

"Okay..." His brow pinches. "That's a good thing, right?"

My half smile causes him to breathe. "Yes, a very good thing." The wrinkles across his forehead disappear. "The even better news is the syndrome is curable, easily treatable, and has a rapid recovery time frame. Completely eradicated in four to six weeks."

"Oh my god, Angie, this is amazing." His smile fades once he reads my face. "There's more?"

I nod.

"That's why we're up here as opposed to having this discussion in the room with Floyd?"

I nod again. "The treatment is a drug cocktail. It's simple, and after the first dose, the rest can be administered at home as an outpatient." I bite my lip as my gaze lowers, avoiding his eyes. "The cocktail includes a drug called dexamethasone, which is a potent steroid." I wait for his reaction.

"So?" Brayton shrugs without making the connection. I pause and let it sink in. "The draft."

I nod. "The treatments run four to six weeks. We need to file an updated physical with the baseball league in order for him to be cleared medically for the draft. The latest we can do that exam and file the report is in three weeks. Even if Floyd is a quick healer and somehow completes the treatment in half the time, there will be a high likelihood that the steroids will still be in his system at the time of the exam."

"But it's a medically prescribed steroid for his condition. It's not a performance-enhancing one. Surely there must be an exception process or something." His voice fills with hope, and I feel bad I'm about to crush it.

"We've thought of that as well. Dr. Morgan worked overnight, reading through the league's policies, and researching other sports. They require an approved medical exception for each individual drug. This one is not on their approved list, and no pending exception is in place. We can file for an exception, but their processing time currently is around twenty months." I try to remain calm and use a neutral voice so that Brayton doesn't bounce off the sky. My personal thoughts about the policy don't matter; these are the rules by which we must operate.

"That's insane. There must be another way. This is his entire future, and it will all come down to a matter of weeks. This is beyond absurd." The veins in his neck throb as he begins to pace. I give the time for him to process, his reaction similar to Reggie's and mine.

"Wait, you said if he's a quick healer, there is a chance the steroid may be out of his system in time for the draft. What sort of chance?"

"There is no guarantee, and it's a very slim chance." I sense his attempt to hang on to anything. I won't deceive him.

"How slim, Angie?"

"Less than five percent chance."

"Is there anything we can do to improve those odds?"

I shake my head. "I'm already factoring in his age, his good health up to this point. We'll give him some dietary guidelines for healthy eating, avoiding certain foods and, of course, alcohol. But even with all that at best, it's five percent."

Brayton's eyes snap back and forth as he searches for other options. "And there aren't any other solutions."

"None that I would advise," I start, and I hear Reggie's voice in my head. Treat him like any other patient, lay out all the alternatives, the good and the bad, and let him choose. But for the first time, I must admit to myself he isn't just any other patient. Brayton has penetrated my defenses, and I care for him, for his son, for their future.

"I want to hear them."

I bite my lower lip, afraid to speak. If this was any other patient, I would spit out the choices, lay out the pros and the cons, and wait for them to choose. But this is not the case. Only the prodding of Reggie's voice in the back of my head pushes me to speak, and I'm grateful he's not here. I need to go through this process and face my truth. See what actions I will take when push comes to shove. Will I be brave enough to speak up and treat Brayton like any person under my care?

"Two other options. Both have significant downsides. Option one is to not to treat Floyd with the cocktail until after the draft. It would mean he'd be on restricted activity for the month. Chances are his bone density will continue to deteriorate, and there would be a high likelihood that he suffers another fracture or, worse yet, a break." I try to keep my tone flat, but I am dead set against this option. There is too much risk to Floyd's long-term health. "If he stays on bed rest, he may avoid any further injuries, but keeping a seventeen-year-old on bed rest for that long seems..." I can't complete the sentence.

Brayton squeezes his eyes shut tight, half twisting away from me. The thought of locking his son down for a month is unbearable. I want to stop; I don't want to inflict any further pain, but I have to do my job. I must tell him everything. "The longer we go without treatment, the less confident we'll become for a quick or even full recovery. It'll get him to the draft unencumbered, but if the team that drafts him performs a physical or needs him to report for baseball activities shortly after the draft, his illness will be exposed. This is a high risk..."

Brayton shakes his head. "I won't risk his health, Angie. You know that." I exhale. Thank god. My heart told me this would be Brayton's reaction, but my head warned me to be prepared. Many a person has principles until pushed into a corner.

"The other option isn't much better. We begin treatment on Floyd but stop after two weeks. Hopefully, the drugs will stop any further deterioration. We then give his system time to flush the steroids. He'll be able to enter the draft. Right after, we'll need to restart the treatment. Once again, however, when we stop the treatment, we run the risk of the disease activating, wreaking damage. He'll need to be on restricted movement to lower the risk of breakage, and we'll still run the same risk post-draft of a team performing a physical or having him report to a baseball camp." This option is not any better than the first. It reduces some of the medical risk but only for a short period.

Brayton drags his hand across his chin as if pondering this choice. I hold my breath, praying he sees the danger of this option.

"I can't in good conscience consider any plan that places his health at risk. You've done your job; you've located the cause and found a cure. It's time for me to do mine—to protect my son and have him get the best treatment possible and get him healthy. That's all that matters." Brayton looks at me, not with anger or sadness or weariness but relief. He truly only cares about getting his son healthy.

He truly is a man of his word and a tremendous father. "Thank you, Angie, for this, all of this. Let's start the treatment."

I nod. "I know how much this decision is costing you, Brayton, but it's the right one for both of you."

He pulls me into a hug and places a warm kiss on the top of my forehead. "It's the right one for all of us."

I'm touched by his words with the focus on finding the root cause of Floyd's disease. Brayton and I have had little time to discuss us. My fear is that once Floyd had a clear path forward, they would disappear back to Springfield.

Brayton's words tell me he does see a future. I just don't know how it will work.

Chapter Twenty-Two

My nervous hands shake as I insert the key to my condo after a long day. Reggie joined me in the late afternoon, and we gave the first treatment to Floyd. The minor procedure went well, and he's being observed overnight before his discharge in the morning.

Dad completed his world tour around the hospital, visiting colleagues and former coworkers. He stopped by at the end of his visit to invite me to an impromptu happy hour, which the doctors insisted on. I declined but was happy to see such a bright smile on his face.

Tomorrow, Brayton and Floyd will leave the hospital and head back to their home. But before that happens, I have one final night with him.

"You okay?" His deep voice steadies me from behind, followed by a slight squeeze of my shoulder to let me know he understands the significance of this evening.

I give him a tentative nod and push through the door. It's only eight thirty in the evening, yet it feels so much later. Brayton met me in the lobby after the end of visiting hours. I waited for him with a go bag of goodies prepared by Chef Marian, who was floating over the moon when my dad dropped in on her. She somehow thinks I am responsible and rewarded me with a stack of fresh-baked cookies.

"Why don't you get comfortable, and I'll set the table," Brayton suggests, and I get the sense he's up for a quiet evening as well. I mouth the words *Thank you*, not sure if I have the strength to speak it out loud. I disappear into my bedroom and drop to the edge of the bed. I throw my head back and lay out flat, overwhelmed by the thousand thoughts in my head.

Relief that Floyd is on his way to being healthy. Grateful Reggie didn't listen to me and called Dad. Today's conversation was the best one we've had in almost a year.

Yet concern floods my veins, a sense of doom on the horizon. There is no way Floyd qualifies for the draft with steroids in his system. Their entire future and lives will be negatively impacted because of the medical clearance report I have to file. It's not lost on me that it will be me who puts the dagger into the heart of the plan they have been working on for years.

And then there is Brayton.

He is sweet, he is kind, he is patient. He's a great father. But he lives in another state. What will become of us? Every time he travels with his son in the future, will I put myself through the petty thoughts of him sitting in another bar in another city without me? Who will be sitting on that barstool next to him? Who will be dancing next to him at the honky-tonk bar in the middle of nowhere?

Am I strong enough to deal with this? Any of this? All of this?

I just need a moment to gather my thoughts and my strength. My hands pull a pillow to my core, and I curl into a ball on top of the bedspread. *I just need a minute* is my last thought before my eyes close and I drift away.

Soft kisses rain down my cheek, waking me from my sleep. Brayton's beautiful profile fills my blurry eyes, and I reach a hand toward him.

"Hey, sleeping beauty, you must be starved. I let you sleep for a bit because you were exhausted, but it's nearly eleven. You must eat something." He gives my hand a slight tug, which I resist.

"I can have it for breakfast. I'm hungry for something else right now." I pull him onto the bed. His knees land on each side of me, straddling me.

His brows pinch, his gaze intense. "You sure? I thought we were going to talk..."

"In the morning, we use our words," I plead. "Tonight, our bodies will do the talking." I push up on my elbows, our noscs touching. "Make love to me, Brayton." I hear the desperation in my voice, the yearning. My heart pounds against my rib cage, a beat telling me I need this connection as much as I need air.

His dark eyes swirl with a look no man has ever shown me. "Love?" he asks, knowing the significance of my phrase.

"Yes, love. One last night—for us."

He places a quick peck on my lip as I ease back onto the bed. "Angie, please know once we do this, it isn't just for one night. We'll figure it out, but it's forever. Is that what you want?"

My hand rises to cup his face. Heat fills my chest, and water fills my eyes. "More than anything in the world." I trust him when he says we'll find a way. He is a good man, a man of his word.

We move slow, purposeful, two people attuned to what is occurring, both aware of the significance that this is Brayton's last evening in Eastport for some time. Two people committed to a future that is too murky to see clearly in this moment. Two people with a need to express through their bodies how they feel toward the other.

Our kisses are softer, our touches more deliberate, our bodies moving with heightened awareness. The bedroom remains dark enough to hide the tears in my eyes, the thunder outside loud enough to cover up my sniffles.

Rain pelts the windows, the wind whipping up a frenzy. I ignore it all and focus on the man in my arms. The man who can see a future I don't. The man whose future I hold in the palm of my hands. The future I will have no choice but to destroy.

Brayton keeps me in stitches as he unloads a barrage of dad jokes over breakfast. We both attempt to avoid the heaviness of the morning for as long as possible. But it's unavoidable.

During cleanup, with time running out, we have no choice but to dive in.

"I can be back here in Eastport every weekend," Brayton plunges right in. "Floyd will be on restricted activities, and I will have him on lockdown at the house until after the draft. I can have my sister babysit one weekend, and I can have him spend a weekend at some of his friends' the other weekends," he rambles.

I snicker at his attempt to take it all on his shoulders. "You don't have to do that. We're not insecure teenagers. We can survive a weekend or two without seeing each other," I start. "We have FaceTime and phone sex," I tease. "And I can come to Springfield too. I'd love to see your place." I attempt to keep it light. "We don't have to figure it all out at this moment. We've already covered the most important decision. We want to be together. That's all that matters to me." Just saying the words I never thought I'd say causes my throat to catch. "Thank you, Brayton, for coming into my life."

He pulls me into a hug, and I press my face into the crook of his arm. "I'm the one who should be saying these words. Because of you, Floyd is going to have a healthy future. That's all I can ask."

He's opened the door, so I run with it. "If there are steroids in his system when I test him before the draft, there will only be two options. File the report with the steroid finding and or have Floyd drop out just prior to the draft and we try to control the narrative. Both options suck, sorry." It hurts for me to say the words, but as his doctor and his friend, he needs to know what's ahead.

He nods. "I know. He'll be devastated, but we'll manage. We always have. Us Pattersons are a tough breed." I feel his squeeze tighten, and I sense the tension of the draft once again. "Just like the Carmichaels," he jokes, attempting to lighten the mood. "If it comes back positive, we'll drop out. At least with us dropping out, there is an outside chance of a qualified college picking him up. By the time we decide on a school, he'll be off the medication, and they can run all the tests in the world on him." Brayton tries to hide the disappointment in his voice as he lays out the backup plan. What he fails to mention is what will happen to their home or how they will pay for college if Floyd doesn't get a scholarship.

I twist up and place a soft kiss on his lips. "I think we should start to get ready to head into the hospital and see how Floyd's night went."

Brayton returns the kiss and whispers, "Not nearly as great our mine."

How did I wind up with this wonderful man? "Why don't you hop in the shower first. I'll finish the cleanup here."

"You sure you don't want to join me?" he teases.

I smack the side of his arm and shoo him away. "If we go down that road, we'll never get out of here." I unapologetically stare at Brayton's tight rear as he disappears down the hall. Once gone, I grab the two coffee cups from the table and walk toward the sink. I notice the stack of magazines Brayton had carried with him from the hospital. He's probably bought every magazine in the gift shop to read as he sat by his son's bed. I notice the colorful, odd-shaped brochure that he had buried in the hospital chair yesterday.

Curiosity gets the better of me as I stride toward the pile. The sound of the shower emboldens me as I lift a sports magazine and peer down at the brochure. Bright yellow letters across a scenic campus background make it unmistakable—Eastport College. Why is Brayton looking at brochures for a local college? If he's looking for Floyd's benefit, why wouldn't it be for one of the large southern schools that have an advanced baseball program?

It takes a second for me to make the connection. Brayton never got to go to college. He stayed home to raise Floyd. With Floyd getting drafted and having a signing bonus, this is his opportunity to go away to college and fulfill a promise he made to himself so many years ago. And out of all the schools in the country he could escape to, he's looking right here in Eastport. There can only be one reason.

He wants to be close to me.

I flip through the pages, Brayton's doodles on the margin, notes to himself confirming my theory. He's circled the degree in architecture. It's a perfect complement to pair with his construction background.

Part of me swoons with just the thought that after only a few days of knowing me, he is so confident in our future he's planning on moving to Eastport. The other part of me feels the weight of what this means. The draft means even more than I ever imagined for this family. It's not just Floyd who has been working hard for a dream deferred. The draft outcome now holds Brayton's future as well.

Everything is riding on Floyd being able to apply for the draft. Even I know putting all your eggs in one basket is a poor strategy, but it's the only one we have.

Chapter
Twenty-Three

I feel the disapproval rolling off Reggie's shoulders as he shadow steps behind me. I focus my grip on the wheelchair and push a beaming Floyd out the front door bay exit leading to the parking garage. Brayton holds open the door, a wide grin on his face. It flickers from his son up to me and back down.

Their late-model Toyota idles at the curb as I place my hand on Floyd's shoulder, holding him in place. Nearly every patient, eager to get away from the hospital, looks to hop out of the wheelchair and race to their vehicle the moment they inhale the fresh air of freedom. It's like a prisoner being released after a long term. The immediate reaction is to run before someone tells them there's been a mistake and they must return inside.

But hospital policy and, yes, rule dictates that hospital personnel escort the patient all the way to their vehicle.

Brayton races ahead and pulls open the passenger door and then turns to help his son out of the wheelchair.

"Dad? Is all this necessary? I feel fine," he protests.

Brayton shakes his head and wraps an arm around his son's shoulder and helps him into his seat. When he leans in to secure the seat belt, Floyd pushes him away.

A giggle escapes my lips as I know the doting father routine is only beginning. At our discharge review this morning, I reminded them that Floyd will remain susceptible to fractures and breaks at least for the next two weeks until the drugs have time to work their way into his immune system. Reggie and I recommended bed rest for the next week, restricted to the house over the following one, and then minimal physical activities, nothing more active than a slow walk, over the two following weeks.

Floyd railed against the restrictions, but Brayton was all on board. As we left them to complete the discharge paperwork, he was already forming a long list of bad movies for them to watch along with threatening to teach him how to play every card game known to man.

"We're going to be okay, thanks to both of you." Brayton appears in front of me, a joy in his step and a smile on his face.

Reggie steps next to me, placing a hand on the back of the empty wheelchair. "Stick to the drug regiment, don't miss a dose. Vitamins and lots of leafy vegetables. We'll see you back here just prior to the draft for the follow-up and pre-draft clearance tests."

Brayton nods in Reggie's direction before his gaze shifts to me. Heat trickles down my neck, and I already know where his mind is racing. We talked about this goodbye this morning. This public goodbye in front of the hospital with my colleagues looking on and his son in the car. Although we both are not hiding our relationship from anyone, we jointly agreed to keep the farewell tame.

Prior to the start of my shift this morning, we said a private, intimate, damn near R-rated goodbye in my office.

"Precious cargo there." I jerk my chin and wave an arm toward his car. "Drive safely, and text me when you get home."

His gaze flickers up to the hospital for an instance. "Trust me when I say we're happy to be leaving this place, but we are kinda going to miss it. I miss you already." His lips pucker and blow me an air-kiss.

I lean forward into a hug and bury my face in his neck. I take a long inhale, knowing I will miss his fragrance all over me in the coming days. "My bed already misses you," I whisper and place a kiss on his warm cheek.

"Keep it warm until I return," he teases. "We got this, all of this." He nods and takes a step back, his penetrating glare inspecting my reaction. It remains that way as he steps backward around the car until he reaches the driver's door.

"Go do more good," he shouts before his hand pounds on the top of the car, hitting it twice. He disappears behind the wheel, toots the horn twice, waves, and pulls away.

I stand there, feet locked in place, feeling like a teenager whose prom date just dropped her off for the evening. My gaze follows the rear of the car all the way out of the parking lot and past the turn to the service road, until it disappears around the bend.

I turn, surprised to find Reggie still standing next to me, a mere six inches separating us. His lips are pinched tight and flat, disapproval written across his face.

"Under what scenario will Floyd not show steroids in his system when they return for the pre-draft clearance tests?" He doesn't waste time with the question that has been sitting on his tongue all morning.

I shake my head. "I know it's a low probability. You heard me explain it to the both of them." I flip up the foot holders on the wheelchair and twist back toward the hospital.

"Yet they both seem to believe they will beat the odds. You led them to believe that because he's an athlete and he's young. We both know that is not the case. That's not how science works."

Reggie holds open the door, and I push the wheelchair through. "Their family has been through enough, Reggie. They are going to be sacrificing so much over the next few weeks. Floyd is going to miss the next three weeks of being with his friends, confined to his house during one of his last months as a senior in high school. Do you know how hard that's going to be? Brayton is adjusting his entire work schedule to work from home to care for his son. They needed something positive to believe in to help get through these next weeks." I spew my prepared reasoning, expecting this challenge from Reggie.

"You're not helping them, and you know that. You're giving them false hope that will only sting harder when he doesn't qualify for the draft." Reggie presses the elevator button before turning to me. "I think I'll take the stairs." Fire blazes in his eyes. "And for the record, you're not fooling anyone with your contrived rationale. You have given them hope because your medical opinion has been overtaken by your relationship with Brayton. It's clouding your ability to be unbiased, just as I feared."

Before I can respond, he turns, and all I see is his back, his white lab coat disappearing through the stairwell exit. The elevator dings, and I push into the crowded car, people scattering to the sides. I twist the wheelchair as the doors close, and a nurse by the control panel asks, "Where are you going, Doctor?"

"Down," I reply.

"Which floor?" she asks for clarification.

I whisper my response. "As low as it can go."

Chapter Twenty-Four

I can't believe it's been two weeks. Two very long, very different weeks. It's incredible Brayton and I had only spent a few days together, yet he had somehow embedded into every part of my life.

Walking to work will never be the same, striding hand in hand, taking in the sunshine. His optimistic outlook brightened my morning and was the absolute best way to start my day. Checking in on Floyd multiple times a day just to get a sneak peek at Brayton. A quick lunch together, a stolen rooftop kiss, an intimate dinner, and, of course, the overnight.

Not having him around has been torture. I've tried to bury myself in work, extending my workday, but I could only do that for so long.

We've chatted every night. He's somehow pulled me into an online game night with him and Floyd one evening. As promised, Brayton and I FaceTimed and had phone sex. It was incredible and much hotter than I ever thought it would be. But it will never compare with the real thing.

Which is why I'm driving eighty-five miles an hour toward Springfield. I left directly from the hospital, a weekend bag in my trunk, and Brayton on my mind. I press the display panel on my rental car and have it dial Brayton. He picks up on the first ring.

"You here already?" I love the excitement in his voice. He's looking forward to this nearly as much as I am.

"I'm turning the corner now. See you in thirty seconds." My lips pull wide into a smile that has been splashed across my face the entire drive. I was pleasantly surprised with the flow of traffic, expecting more resistance on a Friday evening. With me speeding, the one-hundred-mile drive took me less than ninety minutes. I take it as a good sign of what is to come this weekend.

The block is a quiet stretch of modest single-family homes with small yards. I check the house number and pull into the driveway. The house is a cute two-story A-frame home, like every other home on the block. The siding is powder blue with black trim, and even from where I sit, I can tell it is very well maintained. The grass is cut sharp, a low row of hedges across the front walkway leading to the house. I take in the white door with a gray screen door, expecting Brayton to come rushing through it any second.

His deep voice surprises me from behind. "There you are, beautiful." He appears at the end of a path next to the garage, coming from the rear of the property.

He's wearing a dark T-shirt covered by a blue-and-gold apron with the local baseball team's logo on it. His bare legs peek out of his shorts covered by the apron. His eyes sparkle with glee, and my heart skips a beat. I've missed this man.

"I've missed you so much," I whisper and leap into his arms. He wraps them around me, and I press my lips to his. I need to feel him, to breathe him, to taste him, to know that he is real. That he is mine.

My feet lift off the ground as he picks me up, showering me with kisses down my collarbone and returning to my lips. I wrap my legs around him, and he slips a hand beneath my dress, squeezing my rear. My schoolgirl screech of joy must nearly blow out his eardrums as he almost drops me. I don't relent, our lips remaining locked, his hand caressing my face, our tongues reuniting. He feels damn good. "You have no idea how much I've missed you... this... everything."

He takes me by my hand and leads me down the path on the side of the house. Painted golden bricks dot the green grass. "Follow the yellow brick road," he chuckles. "One of Floyd's favorite movies growing up."

This little gesture warms my heart. I follow him, hopping from brick to brick like a modern-day Dorothy. When we get to the backyard, Brayton releases my hand and waves an arm toward a chair. Not just any chair, but a high-back Adirondack chair housing his son, Floyd. Floyd is seated with a goofy smile on his face, covered from his chest down to his toes in bubble wrap.

I burst into a laugh that floats up into the beautiful blue sky. I approach Floyd and lean down, giving him a hug, the crinkling of plastic against my shirt causing us both to laugh.

"I convinced Dad to wrap me. I figured you'd get a kick out of it," Floyd says between laughs.

We both twist to face Brayton, who stands six feet away with a proud smile on his face. "He's been doing great. The medicine is working, but we're not taking any chances."

"This is the furthest I'm allowed out of the house," Floyd says, pointing to the sliding doors four feet behind him. "But I'm okay with it. Only a few more weeks left."

Floyd's eyes glaze over, and I know he's thinking about being on that baseball field again. "Soon," I whisper.

"Get comfortable." Brayton points to the chair next to Floyd. "I have to tend to the grill. I hope you worked up an appetite on the drive."

For the first time, I notice the pillow of smoke from the grill on the far side of the backyard. There are two grills along the property line, a standing black Weber charcoal grill filled with vegetables—corn, peppers, onions, and mushrooms from what I can see. Next to it, running alongside the fence, is a custom-built red-and-black brick gas grill with two burners and a minifridge. Both grills are working overtime, smoke billowing up into the purple-blue sky.

"Dad takes his grilling pretty serious." Floyd beams and sticks out an arm, nodding toward his wrist, where the bubble wrap is secured with duct tape. "The scissors are on the table there." He directs me to the small table next to his chair, a plastic jug filled with water and a roll of tape sitting there.

As I cut the tape, I steal a glance over my shoulder at Brayton. Next to the grill and connected to the fence are a set of outdoor speakers. A light country tune streams. Brayton's feet move in a dance pattern as he rearranges barbeque chicken with the tongs. The song takes me back to our country line dancing excursion.

"I must say—" I cut off the tape from Floyd's other wrist, and he begins to unwind the bubble wrap from his arm. "—you have to be the model patient. Most teenagers would be sneaking out of the house, going to senior-year events, and not taking their medicine."

I don't expect a response, but Floyd surprises me. "It's the least I can do." I look up from cutting the tape on his right ankle, my gaze imploring him to explain. "Dad has sacrificed so much for me."

I give him an understanding nod, but Floyd shakes his head and looks over toward the grill with a twinkle in his eye. "We're so close, and I've never seen him happier. Thank you."

I shake away the compliment.

"Dad used to work construction when I was young. He'd prepare my breakfast and lunch the night before and would have a neighbor come over to the house at five in the morning to sit with me when he went to work. The neighbor would put me on the school bus, and my dad would be home when the school bus returned at three thirty.

"Just as I was about to graduate from elementary school, he was offered a foreman promotion. It meant much better pay, but the hours would be longer. He would not be able to be home when I got out of school. He didn't want me to be one of those kids shuttled from school to after school, arriving home exhausted in the darkness. He turned down the promotion."

I lean into Floyd, afraid that what he is sharing is a family secret. The smile on his face grows as his gaze remains on his dad, who has his back to us, focused on the grill. "When I got to middle school and began to play Little League, my dad left the construction job and signed on to be a sales rep for the parent company, working remotely full-time, planning new projects, and troubleshooting supply and quality issues. It gave him full control of his schedule and hours. He could work early mornings and late evenings, adjusting his schedule to fit my Little League program. He never missed a game or a practice, but it was more than that. He never wanted me to ever feel like I was missing a parent. He showed up at every parent-teacher conference, every science fair, school trip, bake sale, school production, you name it. He passed on so many promotions at work, just so he could be there for me."

Floyd reaches across the small gap that separates our chairs, his hand landing on my forearm. "He passed on so many relationships. Women who couldn't deal with his priorities, women who didn't want to get involved with someone else's kid. Good women who my dad pushed away because he wanted to focus on my needs."

I try to steel my reaction. There isn't any aspect of Brayton's life he hasn't sacrificed to provide everything for his son, even when it comes to partners. Floyd has unknowingly provided an answer to a question that had lingered in the back of my head: how such a wonderful man like Brayton had remained single this long.

Floyd's voice snaps me out of my trance. "So if I have to stay home for a few weeks so that there is a possibility my dad can finally see that I'm good and he's okay to go live his life, I will do that. My dad has done everything possible to make sure I'm happy. It's my turn now. He likes you, Dr. Carmichael. I hope you like him."

A warmth rushes from my chest to my cheeks, and I feel the emotions about to take over. I push it down and give him a steady nod. "I do. A lot," I whisper.

"Hey, hey, I hope my boy isn't talking your head off," Brayton says, approaching. He's carrying two skewers with a piece of barbeque chicken poking out the end of each. "He's excited to be talking to someone other than me. I brought you a quick taste. Dinner will be ready in about ten minutes."

Brayton hands Floyd his skewer, but he holds mine above my head, forcing me to rise from the chair. He holds the tip, dangling the morsel in front of my mouth. He stares down at the skewer, his gaze landing on my lips as I take a bite.

"Oh my god, that is delicious, Brayton." The crispy bite is packed with smokey flavor and just the right amount of char. "You should open up a restaurant."

His chest swells with pride. "Ten years messing with a garbage can DYI barbeque pits at construction sites will teach you a thing or two."

Before I can react, he gives me his back as he races back to the grill to tend to the feast he is preparing.

Every minute I'm around Brayton, I find out something new about him. Something that makes him even more appealing. I continue to stare as he nears the grill, entering the range of the speakers, and begins to side shuffle to the music I can't hear. He's a teddy bear of a man with a heart of gold.

I press my hand to my chest and stare in his direction and appreciate the moment that I let go and let myself fall.

Chapter Twenty-Five

I 've never met a man like Brayton before. It's a simple statement yet so profound. I watch him from the foyer near the front door as he hugs Floyd from over the back of the couch. Floyd holds a video game controller in one hand and pushes his dad off him with the other, both of them laughing like teenagers.

Sitting on each side of Floyd on the couch are two of his friends from high school, Leon and Travis. Their overnight duffel bags sit on the floor, where they threw them the minute they arrived.

"Okay, boys, remember no roughhousing or leaving the house," Brayton reminds them for the tenth time.

"Just go already," Floyd says, turning to the television, where a massive explosion fills the screen. "You made me crash," Floyd says, passing the controller to Travis. He juts his chin in my direction. "Your lady is waiting for you." He shares a knowing smirk with his father before waving in my direction. "Good night, Dr. Carmichael."

I wave back, not wanting to say too much. Floyd's friends do not know anything about his injury or me treating him. The family has gone with the plausible story of an overprotective dad putting his overeager teenaged son on house arrest to keep him from doing anything stupid this close to the draft. His friends seem none the wiser, and Brayton, being an overprotective dad, is not far off-brand.

He approaches me and wraps an arm around my waist, pressing his lips to the top of my head. I can't believe how good this simple gesture feels. We no longer need to hide our feelings or relationship like we did in the hospital.

His lips nibble my ear, and he whispers, "I know I told you getting a hotel room wasn't necessary, but now that you are here, I'm really glad you insisted."

I peek over his shoulder at the boys, who are all engrossed in their video game. I slide my hand from his waist and give a gentle squeeze to his backside. "I've been waiting all evening to do this. Wait till we get back to the hotel, and I'll show you what else I've been waiting to do for the last few weeks."

Brayton's hand slips into mine, and he shouts over his shoulder, "Good night. I'll see you in the morning." He pushes me through the door, not waiting for a reply. "I'm sure you've done enough driving for the day. I'll take over."

We walk hand in hand to his car. He holds the door open for me, and I watch him hop around the front of the car like an excited teen on date night. I can't help but blush at the feelings welling up in my chest. Brayton not only has me feeling like a kid, but he also has me pondering thoughts I thought I had buried long ago. And based on the grin he gives me when he slips into the driver's seat, he's thinking the same thing.

***

When I booked the hotel room, I did it because I wanted alone time with Brayton. Although we've both committed to this relationship, I thought it wiser to take things slowly when it came to Floyd. There is no need for me to shack up with Brayton at the house or pretend we aren't a couple by sleeping on the couch. Floyd isn't dumb. He knows things between me and his dad are progressing, but he doesn't need to have a firsthand account of it, especially given his condition and inability to leave the house.

I opted for the suite at the hotel, hoping to have more of Brayton's time than just the overnight. Images of us lounging on the couch, cuddled in each other's arms, and getting to know each other at a leisurely pace tipped me to that decision.

As I exit the bedroom's bathroom, I spot the silver-and-red gift-wrapped box sitting in the center of the bed. Brayton sits on the corner chair, shirtless and only in boxers, and I wonder which treat to open first.

"What's this?"

His arms rest on the ends of the chair, his eyes dark and stormy, tracking my every movement. I've slipped on my present to him, a tiny red lace-and-silk slip. The cool material swipes across my legs as I step to the bed, making me feel like a goddess.

"Just a little something to show my appreciation. For making the trip..." He rises, "For all the follow-ups with Floyd..."

The box is the size of a shoebox yet lighter.

"For you being you." I feel the heat of Brayton's body as he presses against me, his lips near my ear. He brushes away some of my hair, his heated breath distracting me. "Open it. I think you'll like it."

I lean back into him, enjoying this playful side of him. "You didn't have to..."

He interrupts me with a kiss on my neck. His lips lock in place, and I wait for a nibble that doesn't arrive. "Someday soon, I will mark you and let the world know you are mine. Until that day..."

My knees buckle, but Brayton doesn't allow me to fall. He's there to catch me. We sit in the comfortable silence for a few beats. Reluctantly, I pull on the black ribbon. It slides open with little effort. I twist to face Brayton, wanting to see his face when I open the box.

Slowly, I lift the top. It only takes a peek for me to know what it is. "No you didn't!" I rip off the top and burst into a laugh that sounds like a young version of me. I reach in and pull out a smaller version of the skeleton I have in my office. This one is wearing a blue-and-gold baseball cap and a customized gray sweatshirt with the words *Dr. Carmichael's Number One Patient.*

"I love it," I say. "This is the sweetest." His kindness and thoughtfulness are so foreign to the experiences I've had with so many other men.

"I was going to wait and have the baseball cap match the team that drafts Floyd, but I knew I would never be able to wait that long. I nearly blurted it out last week when I picked it up. I've been counting down the minutes until I could give it to you. I'm always counting down the time until I see you again, Angie."

His throat catches, and I give him the space to compose himself. This is really happening. It's not just me. We are in this together.

"Thankfully, we are here together now." He blinks away the water in his eyes, and I twist, my gaze landing on my shoulder. "Since I've unwrapped your gift..." My index finger flicks the red silk strap, pulling it to the edge of my shoulder, letting gravity and my movement force it to slide down. "Would you like to unwrap yours?"

He bites down on his lower lip, his finger toying with the strap on my other shoulder. "I may not be as gentle unwrapping my gift as you were with mine." His gaze flicks up to meet mine, a dark swirl of desire battling his movement.

I tip up on my toes and place a ghost kiss on his lips, my hands reaching for the band of his boxers. I whisper the words I know will propel him into action, the words that let him know I want what he wants. "I'm counting on it."

Chapter Twenty-Six

I t's only been a week, but it feels so much longer. Seven days since I left Brayton's arms, stealing a final weekend kiss before ducking into my rental car and driving home. Seven days since we began our countdown until we'd see each other again. The final seven days of us living with the shadow of a plan that has only a limited chance of succeeding hanging over us.

But that's the thing—when someone has crept into your heart, they remain in your head every moment of every day. All week, as Brayton and I talked, texted, and FaceTimed, my mind raced with what-if scenarios to deal with the reality that is about to hit us.

Today is the day of the follow-up appointment and test. The day we find out if keeping Floyd home and shrink-wrapped worked.

Phone in hand, I stand outside the hospital.

The scene in front of me takes me back a few weeks. This time, it's different. Brayton doesn't have to assist Floyd into their car. This time, he's all smiles. He's feeling healthy, able to walk on his own, able to return to school for his last day of classes and graduation this week.

Brayton wraps me in his arms, and I don't protest. We may be at the hospital, and there are colleagues all about, but I no longer care. I know after today our relationship will be tested, and I want to hold on to every second we have.

I tip up on my toes and press my lips into his, the warm, woodsy scent relaxing me. "I should have the results by this time tomorrow," I whisper and try to eliminate the concern racing through my body from my voice.

"It's all going to be good news. I can feel it." His optimistic response floods me with guilt. They've done everything I've asked of them. Floyd hadn't left the house in three weeks. He's eaten platefuls of leafy vegetables and organic fruit and has stayed off any processed foods for nearly a month. Hell, at the barbeque, the kid skipped even the delicious lemonade, choosing to drink water. He's a principled kid, just like his father. Brayton has regulated his medicine better than a hospital nurse, each dose delivered down to the second.

They've trusted me and followed my instructions to the letter, and I doubt it will be enough. I blink and look away from Brayton's hopeful eyes, burying my head against his chest. Guilt floods my veins, Reggie's words echoing in my head all week. Did I give them false hope? Were my medical decisions compromised by my feelings for Brayton?

The buzz on my phone reminds me that I'm a liar. I squeeze Brayton hard one last time.

"It's going to be okay, Angie," he reassures me. *Me.* I'm the doctor, and I should be providing the comfort as he and his family face this tremendous obstacle, but I don't.

"Drive safely. I'll call you tomorrow the minute the results are in." I say the words to his chest, unable to look him in his eye.

Brayton places a kiss on the top of my head. "We'll be waiting by the phone." Our eyes connect for a beat, and my lips part. Words I should say get stuck in my throat. The left corner of his mouth crinkles up into a smirk. "You don't have to say it. No matter what, we'll figure it all out as a family."

I place my hand over his enormous heart and purse my lips shut. There is no response to his words. He sees a future, one I so desperately want as well, but it will all hinge on something that is outside our control.

As he steps away to the car, I squeeze the phone hard. The notification I received seconds ago is the first wave of the test results. The most important part, the one I asked the head of the lab to rush.

I wait until the car has disappeared, and I take a long exhale. I want to remember this moment. The point in time when things changed.

I hear the approaching footsteps, but it doesn't register. "What the hell are you doing, Angie?"

The voice I recognize, and the tone doesn't surprise me. People don't appreciate being manipulated. It's Dr. Morgan.

"Reggie? What are you doing out here?" I twist to steal a final glance toward the exit, Brayton's car long gone.

When I turn back, Reggie is pointing over my shoulder. "So that was them, huh? It's true? I didn't believe Nurse Reynolds when she asked me if I was meeting with you and the Pattersons this morning. She heard from Nurse Chin they were here."

I lower the phone next to my hip and allow him to rant. He has every right.

"I checked my calendar, and sure enough, there is no follow-up visit on it for the Pattersons. When did you delete it?" He stomps around me. "I thought maybe it was a mistake. I go to check the file. Bam! I'm looking like boo boo the fool. Not only has my access been revoked—again—but the case record in the directory has my name completely removed as if I never existed. What do you think you are doing?"

My chest pounds as I watch a colleague I had worked hard to earn their trust and respect continue to shout all the reasons why I'll never have it again. I flip my phone over and swipe, unable to resist any longer.

I block out Reggie's rant and tap on the attachment. I chew on my tongue and reread the results a second and third time.

Steroid Test Result—Positive.

My chin lowers to my chest, and I close my eyes. The sting of tears wells up behind my eyelids.

"What? What is it?" Reggie's urgent plea breaks through the fog in my head.

I stick out my phone. "Floyd's test results." Reggie takes the phone from my shaking hand and reads the preliminary report.

"Shit... this means..." he begins, and I already know what he's going to say.

"Floyd won't be able to join the draft. His baseball career is over."

Chapter Twenty-Seven

T his news is going to devastate Floyd. That's the thought that keeps popping up in my head as I sit in my office dejected.

Brayton will be heartbroken for his son, but he will marshal up an optimistic front and look to take more on his broad shoulders. He'll double down on work, somehow take out a third mortgage, if that's a thing, and try to pay for one of those expensive colleges with a baseball program. He'll do everything in his power to keep Floyd's dream alive. He'll sacrifice going to college for another four years, always deferring his dream for others.

I feel powerless. Unable to help my patient, unable to take care of the people I care for. Everyone around me is suffering, making sacrifices, and I sit here in my office, throwing my hands up in the air, trying to tell myself I've done my best when I know that's not true.

The Pattersons have played by the rules all their life and look where it's gotten them. I've always known this would be a possibility. I live in the world of science and numbers, and the odds were never in our favor. Especially given the ridiculous rules we were given.

Rules.

Goddamn rules.

They were my father's downfall, and now I realize they are going to destroy my relationship with Brayton.

I stare down at my iPad at the latest update from the lab. The final test results confirm the rushed preliminary ones. Positive.

It's the final nail in the coffin.

The final verdict has been rendered. My next step is clear. I must complete Floyd's follow-up exam report and then prepare the formal report for the baseball reporting authority. It will be Brayton's decision whether I file it or if he withdraws Floyd from the draft. Either choice will kill them. But they're the only plays we have left—that's what the rules dictate, right?

***

I've called in Dr. Jarvis to cover my shift for me as I bury myself in my office, putting together a plan that will probably get me fired.

I glance at the clock on the bottom of my screen. I've been buried in the laptop for nearly two hours. When I hear a knock on my door, I don't bother to look up. "Go away. Dr. Jarvis is covering. I'm not here."

The door squeaks open, and I turn to face the last person I expected to see in my office. "But I can see you," says Reggie.

I assumed after our encounter outside the hospital that he'd never grace the Ortho floor with his presence again. He steps to my desk, brows pinched, and lowers my phone onto the desktop.

"In the chaos downstairs, I forgot to give you your phone back," he says.

I squint in his direction and pick up the phone. "Th... thanks." I hadn't realized I didn't have the phone.

"I see what you are trying to do, Angie. And it's not going to work." He remains standing in front of my desk.

I push down my laptop screen, not wanting him to see what I'm working on. "What are you talking about, Reggie?"

He slips into the chair in front of my desk, "I understand why you deleted the visit from my calendar. Why you've removed my name from the files."

I shake my head. "I really don't have time for this today. I'm working on something important."

"Falsifying a medical report to a reporting authority is not just a fireable offense, it can get you sent to prison." Reggie spits out the truth that has been staring me in my face all morning.

"You don't know what you are..."

"I read the report on your phone," he states. "Or should I say reports?"

Busted.

I feel the heat of guilt race to my face. I press my palms down onto the top of the desk to prevent them from shaking. I don't break rules. I'm merely two hours in, and I'm already exposed. "I can explain," I start. "I removed your name from the files so you can have deniability."

He leans back in the chair, a hand to chest as if a blow had landed center chest. "Wow. Deniability. I must be speaking to the wrong Carmichael." He waves a hand toward me. "Angie, you don't have to do this. Not this way. You don't know how to play this game. You're going to..."

I should feel nervous, but I don't. I only feel the cold steel of righteous indignation running through my veins. "Don't you think I know that? Don't you think I've weighed all the options?" I challenge him, and he freezes.

He leans forward in the chair, his eyes softening. "What I was going to say was you're going to compromise your values." He pauses and lets the words float in the air. The cost of my action is much greater than the guilt of breaking the rules, the toll to be paid every day for the rest of my career. "Let me do it? Hell, it's half expected of me." He scoffs out the last point, and I shake my head.

"This isn't your battle to win. Besides, you're right, it's exactly what they would expect from you, which is why you can't be the one. I'm Miss Goody Two-shoes—they'll never suspect and therefore will never even look twice." I steal a quick glance at the closed door and lean forward. "Dr. Richards told me in confidence there won't even be a review panel for this case. Some change in policy due to the budget."

"And you've never considered it could be his way of setting you up? Why would you trust his word after what he did to your father?"

The mention of my father causes me to pause. I wonder if this was how he felt when he was at his crossroads. "You know who is best at breaking the rules, Reggie? Those who know them inside and out. Those who think like an investigator. I know what they will be looking for and where."

"Let me help," he pleads.

"I have to do this on my own."

We stare at each other for three very long beats before he speaks again. "At least let me consult. It's what us doctors do. Have another set of eyes look over your shoulders and point out things you may have missed. You have to know by now if ever you needed to consult with me, this is the topic. Breaking rules."

My breath shortens, and my nostrils flare as I process his request. He does make a good point. This is my career I'm putting on the line. Having a second set of eyes is the practical thing to do.

"You suck at paperwork," I state and attempt to push back the smile on my face. I fail.

His chuckle eases the tension in the room. "Which is why you are doing the writing. I'm doing the listening. Walk me through the two reports."

I take a deep exhale, a little of the weight on my shoulders the last two hours easing. "You saw in the report that the steroids are still present in the system?"

Reggie nods. "Yeah, and they are at a high enough level that can't be explained away as a lab error or a misreading from a vitamin or supplement."

"Exactly. It's what I feared, but we both knew was probably going to be the outcome. How much of the report did you read?"

"Enough to know there is no way around the final reading."

"Yet there is." I don't know why fooling a system that has more checks and balances than the Pentagon brings me such joy. I point to my phone and nod for Reggie to pick it up. "Take another look."

His fingers swipe, and he pauses and then pinches the screen. "What am I looking for?"

"Whose name is on the report?" I lead him.

He swipes up a few times and pinches open the report again. "Wait... what? You mean you had planned this even before you sent the sample down to the lab? You little rule breaker."

I nod.

"So, you sent Floyd's sample to the lab under the John Doe alias." Reggie begins to connect the pieces. We use John and Jane Doe for unidentified patients when we need lab work prior to verification of their ID, in cases such as the patient arrived unconscious, homeless, or a mentally challenged patient, unable to communicate.

"Now open the second report."

"Yeah, I saw that one. I was confused. How did you get a lab report with Floyd's name on it, and it shows no steroids? I thought for a second you had created a dummy report, but it looks authentic."

"It is one hundred percent authentic." Reggie hands me back the phone, and I swipe. "You can see from the email it came from the lab. It's based on a real sample. The lab has separate monthly reports, which they crossmatch to a patient's file, and the summary reports are sent to the administration. Everything must match up, or it kicks off an audit," I state as if it's a commonly known fact. It's one of the hundreds of mundane rules that exist in the hospital. I'm probably the only person other than the lab manager and the administration that even knows of these reporting requirements.

"I take it back. Maybe you are the perfect person to break the rules." Reggie laughs.

"The sample is of one of my ortho patients. An eighteen-year-old kid with a broken arm from the Tough Mudder event." Reggie is smart, and I don't need to connect the dots for him.

"So that you'd have a steroid-free report to put in Reggie's file..." A look of admiration and respect sweeps across his face. "With this, Floyd can qualify for the draft. This is brilliant, Angie."

His words should ease my concerns, but they don't. I've broken nearly a dozen hospital rules. Losing my medical license is just the tip of the things that can be taken from me if discovered. "It's not brilliant Reggie. It was necessary."

"There is one problem." And just like that, my bubble is burst. "You can't remove my name from the file."

"It's for your own protection," I plead with him.

"I get that, and I appreciate the thought, but it will get you caught." His statement has my full attention. "Too many people know I was on this case. It's in the logs down in the ER, the nurses, the technicians, my notes in the lab for Floyd's initial X-rays. There's too much of a paper trail, not to mention Dr. Richards himself being aware. If my name is removed, it will only cause people to take a harder look at what else in the file is wrong."

"Shit, you're right." I hear the panic in my voice, and I wonder how many other little things I hadn't considered. "But I can't have you go down for something I'm doing."

"I'm sitting here, Angie. I'm not stopping you. I'm an accomplice, and I'm perfectly fine with that. Best partnership I've ever had."

"This isn't a joke, Reggie. We could go to jail. I won't let that happen to you." Reggie begins to speak, and I raise a hand, halting him. "I think I got it. I'll restore the records the way they were, including Dr. Richards's switch to me as primary. I'll have your name removed from the point in time of Floyd's discharge." I nod. "Yeah, that'll work. After that, there was no longer a need to disturb an ER doctor for routine monitoring and a follow-up." The more I think it through, the more it makes for a more compelling airtight story. "That way you are in the clear. Any of the illicit activities are just the ortho physician going rogue. You'll be in the clear. Does that work for you?"

He nods slowly. "It's scary how good you are at getting around the rules. Your dad would be proud."

I get it. I understand now why my father did what he did. "I couldn't," I start. "I've followed rules all my life, but this was so arbitrary, so wrong." I clench my hand by my side. I'm angry at myself for risking so much, angry at the world for forcing me to choose. Angry at an unknown, unseen body of men who create rules without understanding the impact they have on families. "If Floyd takes this exact test a few weeks from now, he passes with flying colors. His future is unencumbered, clear, and bright. A person's entire future shouldn't hinge on the arbitrary timing of a test." My voice stumbles, and I feel the tears well up.

"Does Brayton know?" I expected this question yet am ashamed to provide a response.

"No. I didn't tell him." I close my eyes. "I won't tell him."

When I open my eyes, I'm met with another surprised expression on Reggie's face. "Wow. I didn't expect that."

"He has enough on his shoulders. All his life, he's made sacrifices for his son. For once, someone needs to do something for him and his family." I try to justify my actions. "When I talked to him after we determined the root cause, I laid out all the options to him, just as you and I discussed."

Reggie nods. "I remember. Even the one that delayed treatment to allow Reggie to qualify for the draft."

"Yes." I recall that difficult conversation. The one that was filled with so much trepidation on my end, knowing Brayton's choice would reveal his true nature, what he truly valued in life. "He never once hesitated to do the right thing for his son. He said screw the draft if it risked his son's health for a single minute. It was at that moment I knew he was real. A man of his word."

"A man who when pressed against a wall would still choose the right path." Reggie completes my thought for me.

"Yes. A man worthy of a sacrifice—mine."

"He's a lucky man to have you by his side."

"I'm the lucky one. He's shown me how to live a life of purpose and meaning. Life isn't meant to be lived afraid, worried about rules and what you can't and shouldn't do. It's about living dreams, lifting up others, and sacrificing in the name of love." A single tear rolls down my cheek. "He's given me so much in such a short timeframe. It's time for me to lift some of his burden."

Silence fills my tiny office for a few breaths before Reggie speaks. "When are you going to file the report to the baseball commission with Floyd's eligibility?"

I lift the screen of the laptop. "Working on it now. I'm going to finish it by tonight. I'll do one final pass in the morning and will press send then."

"Send me a copy tonight. I'll give it the once-over to make sure we are bulletproof," Reggie offers, and I make note of the use of the word "we." Even after all I've put him through, he is here, working with me.

"Thank you. That means a lot to me," I say as Reggie stands. I step around the desk and wrap him in a hug. "You are really a beautiful person, Doctor." I toy with his nickname, the phrasing causing his friendly smirk to appear.

"I always knew there wasn't any problem that you couldn't fix, Doctor." We both chuckle as I walk Reggie to the door and wave goodbye.

I close the door and slip back behind the desk. I still have a lot of work ahead of me. I have to complete this report, proofread it five or six times, and then somehow prepare myself to call my boyfriend and lie to him.

Looks like today is the day I break all the rules.

Chapter Twenty-Eight

D r. Jarvis is a godsend. That is my only thought as the dear man gave up his second off day in a row to cover for me.

After sending the report to Reggie last night, I sat on pins and needles all night. Reggie sent his feedback on the report at 5:00 a.m. this morning. He bowed to my brilliance and merely provided feedback on a few minor points in the report.

The report is ready to be sent—all it takes is for me to press send—yet I hesitate.

This is the point of no return. A million thoughts flood my head as I pick apart every decision. Thoughts of my dad, Reggie's words echoing in my head, thoughts of starting a life with Brayton with secrets. It's the right thing to do yet it still feels wrong.

I'm an African American female doctor in Rhode Island. People like me can't make mistakes. We aren't given second chances; we are shown the door or worse the inside of a jail cell.

Then I think of the one person I'm doing this for, the one person every doctor makes the sacrifice for—their patient. Floyd. A teenager playing by the rules, following medical advice to the letter, in a system that is about to punish him. Everything I'm about to do, everything I'm about to sacrifice will clear the path for him—this should be an easy decision yet my chest pounds. My instincts tell me it's still not the right move.

By me following the example of my father I break the rules. Rules that will still stand tomorrow. Even if I get away with the deceit, the stumbling block of a rule will remain thwarting the next doctor threating to ruin the life of the next kid like Floyd. Reggie was right about one thing—doing this will compromise my values, it will change me forever. If I'm carted off to prison it won't just reflect on me, it will be a strike against every black doctor that follows. Not one but two black doctors, related no less, unable to follow rules. Every black doctor who follows will face extra scrutiny.

"I'm sorry," I shout to no one and everyone.

I can't punt the problem forward to the next doctor. I recall the review process, the lists of medications already under review. Floyd isn't the first kid who has faced this dilemma. The prior doctors followed the rules, and their patients were more than likely excluded from the draft. I won't let another kid be put into this position.

I close out the email system without sending the reports. I am my father's daughter, but I will not follow him into the darkness. I will find the light even if it doesn't exist. My first step is to restore the original files and update the hospital records to the correct findings. Floyd's lab shows a positive steroid finding. That is the science. That is the reality of the situation. That is the truth. The truth is a rule that should never be broken regardless of the cost.

I only have a few hours before I have to drive to meet Brayton and I have a lot of work to do, starting with a certain phone call that I never thought I would ever make.

***

After several difficult phone calls, I complete the report to the baseball reporting committee and press send. My breathing remained shallow as I hopped in the car and immediately began to drive to Springfield. When I stopped for gas around seven, I saw the email confirmation from the baseball league. It marked receipt of the report with the date and time stamp.

There's no going back now.

Medical reports are being filed by physicians for every player in the draft over the next three days, and the draft is six days away.

I pull up to the curb outside Brayton's house and check the phone one last time. An urgent email flashes in my email from the head of the baseball league and I take a deep breath. It all comes down to this.

My hand shakes as I read the email, tears filling my eyes. I squeeze my eyes tight and take a long inhale as my entire body shudders. I ignore the two follow up emails below it, Floyd's fate already sealed.

***

I flip down the visor and open the mirror, touching up my makeup and applying lipstick hoping to hide the evidence of my cries. "You can do this," I whisper to myself and step out of the car. My shaky feet lead me up the walkway, and I ring the doorbell. The excited skittering of feet eases my concern that it's too early in the morning.

"Sit and eat," I hear Brayton shout to someone who I assume to be Floyd. "I got it."

I slip my hands into one another and let them hang in front of me as the door opens. His dark eyes light up when he spots me, and that beautiful smile follows. "Oh my, what a beautiful sight."

"Good morning, Brayton." He leans forward and kisses me. "I missed this," I whisper.

He leads me into the house, through the living room and toward the kitchen, where Floyd is sitting at the small table eating bacon and eggs. "Hey, Dr. Carmichael," he says, beginning to stand. I wave a hand for him to stay put.

"I see you've moved on from the egg white and spinach omelets," my voice shakes as I attempt to hide behind my lame joke.

He shows off a grin similar to his dad's. "You have no idea how much bacon tastes even better after not having it for a few weeks."

Brayton laughs from across the room as he turns off the burner on the stove. "You hungry? I can whip up something for you."

I shake my head. "I'm good." I slip onto the chair across from Floyd, and Brayton pulls out the chair next to me and sits. He doesn't say a word, letting me set the pace of the conversation. He's always so attuned to my thoughts and needs. "I have news," I begin.

"We figured," Floyd says with a goofy grin.

I twist to face Brayton, who sports a similar one. "I told Floyd not to be surprised if you expedited the test results and would let us know before he left for school this morning."

Their goofy smiles don't fade, and I feel as if I'm missing something. "What aren't you telling me?"

When Floyd speaks, I maintain eye contact with Brayton. "Dad said if you contacted us prior to school, it would be good news, and if we didn't hear till the end of the day, chances would be it wouldn't be as great."

Brayton completes the mystery for me. "No one rushes to tell someone bad news."

"Ahh," I say, finally understanding their behavior. On the drive over, I played out this scenario ten different ways. Most of them had me stumbling over the words, avoiding eye contact, and feeling like a failure. It won't be necessary.

I turn toward Floyd and snicker. "Floyd, I hope you've kept your calendar clear in six days. You are going to be in the draft."

Floyd leaps to his feet, a smile as wide as I've ever seen on his face. "I'm clean?" he first asks before answering himself, "I'm clean! Dad, I'm clean!"

Tears well up in the corners of Brayton's eyes, causing a similar reaction from me. Floyd leaps across the table and pulls his dad into a hug. "This is really happening," Floyd yells. "We did it, Dad."

"You've done it, son."

Streaks of tears rain down Floyd's happy face as he pulls his dad tight. "No. We did it. We are a team."

I give the pair space and time to celebrate. They've worked so long and so hard for this moment. Just witnessing this proves everything I've done is worth it.

"Oh my god, I can't wait to get to school," Floyd says as his dad pounds him on his back.

"Go get your stuff together," Brayton says as he pulls from the embrace.

Floyd turns to face me and pulls me into a tight hug. "Thank you so much, Dr. Carmichael. You've given this family a future. Thank you."

My words get caught in my throat, but Floyd doesn't notice. He's already disappeared to his bedroom to grab his things for school.

Brayton slips an arm around my shoulder and pulls me in for another tight hug. "Thank you for making the long-ass drive to deliver the news. This is the best news this family has received in a long time." He places a warm kiss on the top of my head. "Can you stay for the day? I'll show you the proper way to celebrate." He winks at me, and I pat him on the chest.

"Sure." My voice lacks the enthusiasm expected, and I feel him tense up next to me. "There is just one thing I need to talk to you about." I slip back onto the kitchen table chair and pat the top of the table for Brayton to sit.

"Is everything okay?" Brayton asks, sitting.

"Great. I've sent the report to the baseball committee. He's all set for the draft."

"But..."

My gaze drops to the tabletop. "No but. Everything is fine. It's just me being anal, that's all. I want you to keep Floyd on the drug regiment for the rest of this week, you understand?"

His right hand lands on the top of mine. "I hear what you are asking, I just don't understand why."

My eyelids flutter as I keep my gaze locked on the back of his hand. "He's done so well with the treatment. I just want to make sure we eradicate it from his system completely. Do no harm."

I lay out the medical mantra, hoping Brayton will read between the lines. We are at the start of our relationship. He's a man who has proven time and time again that his word carries weight. Trust is a huge issue. That his son is the most important thing in his life.

"Congrats on the draft, Brayton. I think you and Floyd should go somewhere to celebrate immediately after graduation this week. I'm sure whichever team drafts him would understand." I speak the words slowly, deliberately knowing Brayton is an empath. He's shown a skill to read me, a skill I'm counting on. At the end of the day, this was too big a decision to keep from the man who owns my heart. A man who values trust above everything else.

Brayton's brow lifts as he puts the pieces together. I brace for the fallout. Even if it all crumbles at my feet, it will be well worth it. My pulse races with the silence, every breath causing my anxiety to rise. Did I do the right thing? Will he hate what I did? Will he hate me? Did I not break the rules only to lose the man?

He takes a deep exhale and lifts my hand, placing a gentle kiss on the back of it. "And how long should this celebration trip last?"

Hope fills my chest as his eyes fill with understanding. "I would recommend at least a week. Two would be better."

Brayton pulls me into another hug. "We'll do two but only under one condition."

I wipe a tear of joy from the corner of my eye. "And what is that?"

"If you join us for the second week."

I ponder the question, already knowing how I will answer it. My only hesitation is my schedule and how many favors I will owe Dr. Jarvis.

The hospital has a thirty-day notification rule for doctor vacation requests. I no longer care. I'm a rebel. "I think that can be arranged." I press my lips to his and inhale the man who has put so much faith in me.

"Thank you for everything you've done, Angie. I can't imagine the true cost of all this to you. I can't say I'm not relieved, but I never wanted you to compromise your values. We'd still be here as a couple even if we had to drop from the draft." Brayton always knows what I need, the words I need to hear, the fears deep in my chest.

"I know." A single tear rolls down my cheek and for the first time today it's a joyous one. "I didn't have to compromise anything.," I whisper.

He runs his hand down my back, a comforting stroke that makes everything I've done worth it. "I'm confused. Did the screening show Floyd as positive?"

I nod.

"And you sent that report to the league?"

"Yes," my throat catches as the whirlwind of the morning catches up to me. "I had prepared false reports and was this close to sending them, Brayton. None of this was fair to Floyd and I was prepared to break the law to make things right for him."

Brayton leans back from me, removing his warm hand, his brow pinching, "I'm confused. You filed a positive steroid report to the league, yet we are still eligible for the draft? Please help me understand."

I love the fact that he doesn't jump to conclusions but provides me a safe space to explain at my own pace in my own way. "It all came down to Floyd and my father." I huff out. Once I made the connection between them my path became clear. "I could act like my dad, break the rules for the benefit of my client. And we would have gotten away with it, Brayton, but you know what? It doesn't help the next Floyd. It devalues what I stand for, and it doesn't force the institutions that have these improper rules to change."

"The needs of the many outweigh..." Brayton begins.

"The needs of the few ... Or the one." I complete for him, the famous quote from Star Trek.

"I love that you are a fellow Trekkie and of course you'd know Doctor Spock." He's such a patient man. Most parents would be on the edge of their seat screaming at me to get to it. He does none of this. He sees my heart; he understands what drives me.

A comfortable silence fills the air which allows me to gather my thoughts. "You and Floyd are good people. You've played life by the rules, regardless of the challenges placed in front of you. You shouldn't be punished for that. I've played life by the rules and shouldn't have to look over my shoulder the rest of my career." I recall fingering the business card for nearly ten minutes before making the call.

"Our Marketing and PR Company is a powerful player in the industry, they take on Fortune 500 and federal agencies regularly. I set up a three-way call with the baseball league office this morning. We explained the issue with their exception process and lack of a clear path for non-performance enhancing steroids. We mentioned the long review process and the exceptions currently stuck in their process and the impact they may have had on other ball players. Only after we got their attention and acknowledgement did we introduce Floyd's name."

I pause and wait for a reaction—he nods and lets me proceed.

"I explained to them that his test results are positive, all the details are in the report being submitted and he'll be through his regiment in a few weeks, well before he would report to any team's facilities. We led with honesty and compassion. We told them his story, the love of the game, the travel baseball, the years of commitment and dedication. How an African American kid like Floyd is exactly the type of ballplayer they should be welcoming to the sport. We gently put the ball in their court but not before hinting about the power of our PR team and how this could go sideways quickly in the court of public opinion."

"Wow," Brayton takes a deep breath to process the whirlwind of information. I can hardly believe it myself.

Just as Dr. Richards had said, Carlton Wilson, the head of the PR firm, took my call even at the early morning hour. His job is used to last second demands, and he had his team ready in under ten minutes. Once he was informed of the possibilities of other kids like Floyd stuck in review purgatory, he was all in. The pieces fell quickly.

"And will they tell the teams prior to the draft that he's positive?" Brayton ask the question I fully expected.

My gaze locks with his, "After the draft they will be changing their policies regarding non-performance steroids publicly. They will not be mentioning Floyd's test to anyone. You are good."

He places a hand on mine. "We. We are good."

I feel my lips part, a smile tugging on the corners.

Brayton clears his throat before speaking, "I can't believe you did all of this for us,"

"I had to do it. And I had to do it the right way, my way." The anxious squirl in my chest finally calms. My head is finally clear. "It wasn't just for you and Floyd. It's for all the kids that follow. Rules don't have to be broken from the outside. You can bend them from the inside too." I think back to the call I made in the car to my dad. I explained to him my approach and implored him to do the same.

He immediately mentioned a half dozen organizations and challenges doctors he's met at conferences have run into roadblocks. By the time I hung up with him he was already strategizing on setting up a series of conference calls to plan how they can begin to chip away at some of the bottlenecks in the industry. The restrictive rules that had served their purpose once but need to evolve with the changing landscape. The pride and excitement in my father's voice was one the best sounds this morning—until Brayton opens his mouth.

"You are an amazing woman, Angie."

I wave a hand at him, "I don't know what to say to that."

He pulls me into another hug, this one tight and loving. Brayton has proven dozens of times already to be an empath. I pause afraid the three words swirling in my chest may slip out. Three words I've not shared with another man in all my years. I gaze into Brayton's deep dark eyes and wonder if he can read me, understand what I am feeling.

He leans over and places a ghost kiss on my lips and whispers, "I know. Me too."

Epilogue

B rayton paces in front of the coffee table, the fifty-inch TV streaming behind him. It's draft day, and I'm sitting on the matching love seat at his home in Springfield. The tension in the air is so thick you can cut it with a knife. My elbows are pressed to the top of my knees, my toes lifted, breath hitched as I take in everything happening in the room.

Floyd sits center couch surrounded by two dozen of his friends. Behind them stands his aunt Andora, Brayton's sister. She's just as pleasant and special as Brayton. On the coffee table in front of Floyd rests his laptop. It's open to a secured web connection, his laptop camera focused on him center couch. He ignores his friends' nervous jokes and pats on the back as silence fills the room and all eyes shift to the television. The baseball commissioner, dressed in a conservative navy suit, white shirt, and red tie, steps to the microphone for the fourth time.

It's like déjà vu, and I'm not sure I can withstand this emotional roller coaster. Every time the commissioner steps to the mic, everyone in the room prays he will call Floyd's name as the next pick. Not even the ever-optimistic Brayton expected Floyd to go number one, yet I saw a flash of disappointment cross his face when he didn't. It was only there a split second, and he was right back to being head cheerleader in a heartbeat.

Three times this has been repeated. Three times the room filled with groans. The draft experts have predicted

Floyd may go as high as number seven and as low as thirty-four. Brayton cringed when he heard the lower number. The bonuses drop off significantly after the tenth pick and are all but nonexistent after twenty.

"Quiet, quiet!" Brayton shouts, his long arms extended as he steps around the table and plops on the couch next to his son.

The room goes silent. The commissioner's throat clearing bounces across the room since the volume has been ratcheted up to fifty. "With the fourth pick of the baseball draft, Milwaukee selects Floyd Patterson from John F. Kennedy High School in Springfield, Massachusetts."

I leap to my feet, my hands coming together, clutching my chest. Brayton pulls Floyd into a deep hug, their heads buried into each other. The rest of the room explodes in cheers and laughs. I feel privileged to be able to witness such a scene. They've worked hard for this. They've sacrificed so much.

I sneak a peek at the television, the celebration in the room being broadcast from Floyd's laptop to the broadcast studio. The image of father and son hugging fills the screen as the bottom of the screen fills with a ticker listing all of Floyd's baseball accomplishments. Most of them are foreign to me. They might as well be speaking Greek. The only stat that matters is the one not listed there. He is healthy, he is safe, and his future is secured.

The television shifts back to the hosts, who are playing a video highlight reel of Floyd in action on the baseball diamond. His smooth movement and grace is apparent even to a novice such as myself.

I barely hear Floyd speak over the noise in the room as the host of the draft program asks him a few questions. Floyd is all smiles and goofy laughs, but the absolute best picture is that of his dad beaming next to him. The lines that have always been present across his forehead are no longer visible. The weight of the world has been lifted off his shoulders. It's the most relaxed I've seen Brayton since we've met. Their family's future is now secure.

A small sense of pride swells in my chest as I've played a small part in that. I've helped the family that has always followed the rules navigate the impossible successfully.

It was a grueling journey that not only tested the ability to navigate rules but tested my personal belief system. This family was placed in an impossible situation that was not of their doing. Arbitrary rules placed by nameless, faceless committees determining they had the power to construct an obstacle course of unnecessary hoops because their rigid structure wouldn't allow for common sense to prevail. It's been a battle, but we've cleared the runway not just for the Pattersons but for every future family like them.

They wrap up the short interview, and the scene on the television shifts back to the talking heads, who pontificate on the next possible selection. The commissioner steps to the podium with the next selection that will change the entire future of another family. Brayton mutes the TV. "Okay, everyone, to the backyard. Let's crank this party up a few thousand notches."

He waves everyone toward the back, where he's prepared a feast worthy of a future sports star. It took lots of convincing, but he finally relented and agreed to have the barbeque catered. On the day of his son's draft, the last thing I wanted to see was Brayton stressing out and trying to prepare food for thirty people. Only when I mentioned the bonus money did he finally give in.

The teens and family friends filter out the room, their arms wrapped around Floyd.

"Congrats. You've done a terrific job, Brayton. You can finally relax." I wrap my arms around his waist, his arm wrapping around my shoulder.

"I don't think as a parent we ever relax."

"I expected that answer." I ease out of the embrace and step to my handbag on the kitchen table. I reach in and pull out an envelope. "I got this for you, for when you come back to Eastport."

The look of surprise on his face is the greatest treat. He's a man who sacrifices for everyone else and never expects anything in return. "What's this?"

"It's nothing much. I just want to take care of you for a change."

He rips open the large envelope and pulls out a half dozen blue-and-white oversized certificates. "You got me spa treatments?"

I fail in suppressing my laugh. All I had to do was give ten minutes of my time to Brooke from Droga Pharmaceuticals to receive the certificates. A small price to pay for the joy on Brayton's face. Part of our discussion covered a change in policy—from now on Brooke's admin will allocate a block of certificates to the hospital, all the of the paperwork completed by her company. All the doctor has to do is check a box on Brooke's tablet and sign to receive the certificate. It guarantees her contact with the doctor and the hospital receives all of the tracking information. A win-win. Reggie was shocked when I showed up at the happy hour and told everyone about the certificate allocations.

"This is actually the perfect gift," Brayton continues. "I have something for you too."

I follow him as he steps into the bedroom. He steps to the mirror on his bureau and picks up a plain white envelope.

My name is scribbled across the envelope, and I rip it open. "I hope you like the beach," he whispers, and inside is a postcard for Miami Beach. "I'm taking Floyd and a few of his friends to Disney World this week. And then I want you to meet us in Miami the second week."

"It's perfect," I say.

"Good," he exhales, and I raise a brow seeking clarification. "I already booked the hotel and got us a suite a few floors away from Floyd's." He snickers before a serious expression sweeps across his face. "There is something else I've been meaning to discuss with you."

"Okay." Despite his tone I keep a smile on my face. There isn't anything that can ruin my mood.

He pulls another envelope his back pocket. My hands float to my chest as I recognize the colors, the same as the brochure I discovered a month ago. He holds up the letter with the logo of Eastport University across the top. He's been accepted to their architecture program starting in the fall. "Oh my god, Brayton, you're going to college? And you've decided on Eastport?" I am truly surprised. Brayton had never mentioned the brochure to me, and as the draft drew nearer, I began to doubt he'd select such a small school when he could now afford any school in the country.

"You know why Eastport," he says as if it's plain as day. "Because of you, Angie."

Cue swoon. I've been falling for Brayton since I spotted him across the bar at the hotel. Every step of this journey, he has proven to be unlike any man I'd ever met. Sexy as hell, smart, confident, loyal, and most importantly has a heart the size of Rhode Island.

I scan the rest of the acceptance letter and pause as my finger hovers over a section. "Wait. It says here you've applied for the dorm. Why would you do that? You have to move in with me. The school is not that far from the hospital. You'll be in classes all day while I'm at work. We can spend our nights together. Please say yes."

His smile sparkles, and he doesn't hesitate. "Yes." He laughs. "I didn't want to make an assumption. But thank you. I didn't want to be the old guy in the dorm sharing a room with three nineteen-year-old kids. I've put in my time already."

We fall into a fit of laughs as Brayton leads me out of the bedroom and through the house. We pause, looking out the sliding glass doors at the festivities in the backyard.

Floyd has connected his phone to Brayton's wireless speakers by the grill, the volume cranked up as high as they go. The backyard is filled with loud laughs, teens dancing, and plates being piled high. It's a celebration Floyd has waited for all his life.

I turn and capture Brayton's prideful gaze on his son. There's more work ahead, different challenges around the corner, but today he gets to rejoice in a job well done. He's put his son in the best possible position to succeed.

All the hard work and sacrifices have been worth it. Now it's Brayton's turn to be pampered. The spa certificates and having him move in with me are just the start.

We continue to gaze out the door at the kids enjoying, and I nudge Brayton with my hip. "Hey, when we get back from Miami, can you join me for dinner in Eastport?"

"Absolutely. What do you have in mind? Back to the farm?"

I shake my head. "No, just at our place. I'm cooking."

He snickers, and I wait for the dig. "You cook?"

My laugh joins his, and I try to think of the last time I cooked a meal from scratch. "Yeah. It's been a while, but you've given me a reason to cook again. Plus, there's someone I want you to meet."

He turns to face me, our eyes connecting. "My dad," I whisper.

The corner of his lips ticks up. "I can't wait." He places a soft kiss on the tip of my nose, and the smile remains on his face.

"What?" I ask, his actions causing a goofy grin to spread across my face.

"You do realize you said *our* place?"

I nod. "Yeah, I know." I knew he'd pick up on it. He knows me so well.

They say don't ask a man to move in with you after a few weeks. They say you must separate your personal and professional lives. They say you can't fall in love with someone in a few weeks. "I know we're bending all the rules. It's sort of our thing."

I no longer listen to *them*.

Daddy would agree.

THE END

Thank you for reading Doctor Fix-It. If you enjoyed this book, please consider leaving a Review. They are the best way for other readers to find their next read. And make sure to check out all of the other books in the Doctors of Eastport General Series.

If you are a fan of small town romance with heart, check out my Lake Hope Series starting with Ryan's Hope: Lake Hope Book One.

Want to keep up with upcoming releases, and monthly giveaways - sign up for my Newsletter.

Info on The Doctors of Eastport General

I hope you enjoyed my book, Doctor Fix-It, which is part of the shared world Doctors of Eastport General.

Would you like to read all of them? Find them here on Kindle Unlimited.

Come on in and meet the ER Physicians, Surgeons, Specialists, Residents, and patients that occupy the rooms and halls of the largest hospital on the coast of Rhode Island. We hope you are ready to fall in love with all the sexy stories that take place inside the walls of Eastport General Hospital.

Doctor Heartbreak by D.M. Davis
Doctor Feelgood by Amy Stephens
Doctor D's Orderly Affair by CA King
Doctor Trouble by E.M. Shue
Doctor Temptation by Syd Ryan
Dueling Doctors by DC Renee
Doctor Sexy by TL Mayhew
Doctor Fix-It by Mel Walker
Doctor One of a Kind by Anjelica Grace
Doctor Casanova by Emma Nichole
Dirty Doctor by Amanda Richardson
Doctor All Nighter by Adora Crooks
Doctor Desire by S.L. Sterling

Acknowledgments

Thank you for taking a chance on me. I hope you've enjoyed the story of Angie and Brayton. This novel is part of the incredible Doctors of Eastport General Hospital Medical Romance series. I had an amazing time working with entire team of talented authors and I highly recommend you follow/support each of them.

- D.M. Davis
- Amy Stephens
- C.A. King
- E.M. Shue
- Syd Ryan
- DC Renee
- TL Mayhew
- Melanie A. Smith
- Anjelica Grace
- Emma Nichole
- Amanda Richardson
- Adora Crooks
- and, S.L. Sterling, the organizer and leader of the series

I'd like to also send a special thank you to my beta reader - Vilma Akins. Her critical insights vastly improved this novel. Vilma is an incredible fan of the genre and I can't thank her enough for all the support and feedback she provides.

Thank you once again. If you enjoyed this story, please share and even better post a review online. It helps other readers locate their next read.

Also By Mel Walker

Mel Walker has been writing fiction most of his adult life. Specializing in Short Stories and Contemporary fiction and Romance Novels. A native New Yorker and life-long frustrated NY Mets fan. He loves to write about ordinary people placed in difficult situations, especially as it relates to their closest relationships.

To keep up to date on all Mel Walker's Novels Visit his website - www.authormelwalker.com. The most up to date catalog will be found on his website and Social media

platforms – scan the QR Code for the most up to date
information. Current Catalog includes:
<u>The Lake Hope Small Town Romance Series</u>

Ryan's Kiss

Aaron's Heart

Jackson's Love

Jason's Hope

Trace's Forever
<u>Standalone Romance</u>

The Amazing Date

Somebody's Heartbreak – A Novella

A Matter of Patience – A Novella

StageFight / Love on the Dance Floor – A Novella (Modern
Day
Fairytale Retelling of the Princess & the Pea)
Kiss You Back
<u>Coming Soon - PreOrders available</u>

Summer Sounds - A Summer in Seaside Romance Novel
The Right Guy - A Fake Romance Novel

Mrs. Right - A Romance Anthology

XOXO - A limited Edition Romance Anthology
MoneyBaller - a Players and Sinners Sports Romance
Fall Back into Love – A Romantic Comedy Collection